To

Elizabeth Kay

MISSING LINK

Other titles published by EPRINT Publishing:

A Death in the Family by Caroline Dunford
A Measure of the Soul by Stephanie Baudet
Spectacles by Pippa Goodhart
This Fragile Life by David Webb

About the author:

Best-selling children's fantasy author Elizabeth Kay has turned her hand to writing mainstream adult fiction. She has a varied writing history from plays to poetry to prose. She's appeared on Breakfast Television and at a number of festivals, including Edinburgh and Hay-on-Wye, and lists 'travelling to obscure destinations' and 'trying not to get eaten by the wildlife' as her hobbies.

MISSING LINK

ELIZABETH KAY

PRINT
PUBLISHING

Published in Great Britain in 2009 by EPRINT Publishing
Blackburn, Lancashire
www.eprint.co.uk

© Elizabeth Kay 2009

A CIP record for this work is available from the British Library.
ISBN 978-1-905637-88-1

Typeset in Great Britain by Educational Printing Services Limited,
Blackburn, Lancashire
Printed and bound in Great Britain by CPI Cox & Wyman, Reading,
Berkshire

For Krzysia

Characters

Spliff – *Missing Link* presenter
Patsy – research assistant (looks after Elspeth on the show)
Jessica Pierce – show contestant
Stuart Miller – other show presenter
Prudence – research assistant (looks after Jessica on the show)
Elspeth – Jessica's friend
Fern Marshall- show contestant
Sandra - research assistant (looks after Fern and Karl on the show)
Marilyn Stark – other show presenter
Nicholas Creed – newsreader
Clive – producer
Doctor Aaron Klein – friend of Jessica's parents
Harry – cameraman
Bronwyn Price (Price the Paint) – Jessica's art teacher
Christine Pierce – Jessica's mother
Simon Tree – previous producer
Annie – one of Fern's clients
Karl Richards – one of Fern's mother's ex-boyfriends
Dermot – one of Fern's mother's ex-boyfriends
Max – one of Fern's mother's ex-boyfriends
Maureen Garvey – Jessica's aunt
Louise-Marie – make-up artist
Andy – crew member
Zoë – Elspeth's mother
Edward Pierce – Jessica's father
Charlie – Fern's ex-husband
Rodney – one of Fern's boyfriends
Doctor Rudolph Myers – a friend of Spliff
Strickland (Potty Noodle) – big boss
Eveline Marshall – Fern's mother

One

Missing Link. Cheap and trashy. Twenty million viewers each week, worldwide. Low-budget sets, and real feelings. Fifty minutes of real joy, real despair, real laughter, real tears. The idea was simple: turn the entire population into snoops, and make it worth their while when they came up with something juicy. Unexpected scandals were even more popular than unexpected windfalls.

This was the run-through.

The title sequence appeared on the big screen at the rear of the set; a car being towed by a truck. The tow-chain snapped and the vehicles parted company, careering off in different directions. The title materialised, and then fragmented.

Spliff grinned. "Hello everyone. It's Saturday the twenty-seventh of June, the year's 2020, and England have been drawn against Karetsefia. Welcome to this edition of *Missing Link*, the investigative chat show, and the last one of the series. My name's Spliff, and as usual I think we've got a few surprises in store. You know the form – two subjects who've never met, their life histories, and an unexpected tie-in at the end . . ."

He broke off, listening to the producer through his ear-piece.

Poor cow, thought Patsy, as she looked at the pale, mousy-haired girl labelled "Jessica" who was sitting on the sofa opposite Spliff. I wonder if she's got the faintest idea what she's getting herself into? I didn't, when I started out as one of his research assistants. But you've got to earn a crust, haven't you? You just don't realise the bread's mouldy when you buy it wrapped in nice shiny plastic. I wonder if Jessica saw Spliff on *The Stuart Miller Show* last week.

Spliff had been sitting between Francine Capra, the singer from *The Basingstoke Bitches*, and Rodney Hobbes, the striker for Man U. Hobbes had been defending his sending off against Liverpool, when he'd kicked the referee.

"Kicking the shit out of people is human nature," said Spliff cheerfully, "isn't it, Hobbes?"

"Surely Spliff," said Miller, annoyed, "you of all people shouldn't be advocating violence in sport. There are kids out there who . . ."

"I didn't advocate it," interrupted Spliff. "I merely said it was human nature. Don't twist what I say."

Francine Capra laughed, and ran her long red fingernails through her long red hair. "That's rich," she said, "coming from someone who twists people's *lives* once a week."

"Oh no," said Spliff. "The twists are already there. I simply narrate them."

"I think *Missing Link*'s a *great* programme," said Hobbes, with real enthusiasm.

Spliff laughed. His voice was the most distinctive thing about him; no particular accent, but rich and dark with an occasional astringency like a shot of neat spirits – a good broadcasting voice, instantly recognisable. "Twenty million viewers agree with you, Rodney," he said smoothly. "How many have we got this evening, I wonder?"

Miller deftly turned the conversation to horse-racing. He started to talk about *Filthy Looker*, the genetically-engineered horse that had won everything the previous season. "Beautiful animal don't you think, Spliff?" he said.

"No," said Spliff, "I don't."

"Oh come on," said Stuart, "poetry in motion."

"Poetry's one thing," said Spliff, "and motions are another. It's the second word that describes what *I* think about the whole business. Do we really have nothing better to do than chop up bits of DNA to make one bloody horse run faster than another?"

"You've got no soul, Spliff," said Francine Capra.

"I know," said Spliff. "I'm an atheist."

Patsy could see that Jessica was sweating. She smiled. Compassion wasn't one of Patsy's strongest suits. She'd clawed her way into TV with Botox, hair extensions and imaginative underwear, and she resented people who'd had it easy because they came from more affluent backgrounds. Spliff hadn't had it easy; everyone knew that. She could see him grumbling to someone and scratching his ear. The camera crew were looking bored, and the sound man seemed to be sulking. There was a fly on the coffee table, paddling in something. Someone appeared with a cloth, and then suddenly it was all systems go again.

Spliff sat down and switched on the boyish smile. "And so, without further ado, let's meet our first subject, Jessica Pierce, a twenty-two year old student from Kingston upon Thames. Say hello to the viewers, Jessica."

"Hello," said the girl, manipulated into the near-cretinous one-word reply.

"So, Jessica," said Spliff, "you've no idea why you're here, have you?"

The girl shook her head, out-manoeuvred again.

"Then let's get started. We'll begin in 1998,

the year of your birth . . ."

A photograph of a large house flashed up on the screen and morphed into a Transylvanian castle – complete with drawbridge, full moon, and bats.

"*The Cedars*," said Spliff. "Jessica's childhood home, and very nice too . . ." He swivelled his chair and glanced up at the screen. Two of the cameramen were laughing. Spliff looked annoyed, got to his feet, and walked off the set.

One of the young and trendy researchers – "Hi! I'm Prudence!" – started dishing out cups of something that went by the name of coffee. The original house was back on the screen now, but there was no sign of Spliff.

Prudence sat down next to the girl on the sofa and said, "Do you watch *Missing Link* regularly, Jessica?"

The girl shook her head.

Jessica had only watched *Missing Link* once, which she was beginning to think had been a mistake. Her friend Elspeth told her it hadn't been one of the good ones; the hairdresser had no sense of humour and the fishmonger had been even worse, with his jokes about eels. Even Spliff hadn't been able to get them to gel.

"What do you mean, you're not going to do it?" Elspeth had shrieked. "They know something *about* you, Jessica, something you don't know yourself. I'd be *desperate* to find out what it was. Perhaps they've unearthed some long-lost relative."

"Unearthed would be right. They're all dead."

"Maybe it's just something silly, funny, you know? They did one once where this writer . . . he'd invented this character, and they found someone just like him, it was uncanny. He had the same lisp, the same frizzy hair, everything. The author looked as though he'd seen a ghost, it was hilarious. Oh come on Jessica, you've *got* to do it."

"What you really mean," said Jessica, "is that *you* want to do it. Have they been in contact with you as well?"

Elspeth bit her lip.

"I see," said Jessica.

"Maybe I shouldn't say this, but they asked me a lot of questions about your paintings. I think they're going to introduce you to a gallery owner or something."

"Don't be silly."

"Supposing I'm right, though," said Elspeth. "*Just supposing I'm right.*"

On the spur of the moment Jessica rang the studio and told them she'd appear, and they faxed her a consent form immediately. She read a bit of it, found the language impossible, signed it and posted it back. Later on in the week she enlisted the help of someone at college to translate the small print; there was no way she could get out of the programme unless she produced a doctor's certificate. After that she'd had a couple of months trying not to think about it, and then, with shocking suddenness, the day had arrived.

Two

Fern rinsed her mouth out under the tap. She had actually been sick, she'd been so nervous.

She could hardly believe it when she got the phone call. Fern Marshall, on television, and on *Missing Link* of all things. She would have loved to crow about it to her mother but the two of them weren't on speaking terms at the moment. It had crossed her mind that whatever the researchers had uncovered, it very probably involved her mother. Fern was hoping that the programme would explain a few things. One in the eye for the secretive old bag.

On the other hand, there was always a chance she'd come into some money. She took a deep breath and looked at herself in the mirror. A white-faced woman looked back at her, bleached hair expensively shag-cut the day before, hazel eyes glassy with fright. She'd come in a day early to discuss her clothes with Sandra, one of Spliff's research assistants. It hadn't helped that Sandra was one of those classy redheads who could climb out of a mudbath and still be the business.

Dear oh lor', thought Sandra, when she first saw Fern. What on earth has the woman done to her hair? She looks like a sheepdog. The pastel clothes don't work either, it's as though someone's run her under a tap and wrung her out. "What do they call that haircut?" she enquired, her curiosity overcoming her tact.

"A shag," said Fern, and sniggered.

On the way back to the dressing room Fern had seen Spliff in the distance, and that was what had prompted the throwing up. She'd had a thing about him for ages, so naturally she'd watched *The Stuart Miller Show*. She'd also watched *On Marilyn's Sofa* the week before.

"You're a graduate of the university of life aren't you, Spliff?" said Marilyn Stark, the rather starchy, grey-haired host. "Didn't like school?"

"Hated every minute, sweetheart. Bunked off every chance I got."

Marilyn tried not to prickle at the word *sweetheart*. It was a word she particularly hated, according to a poem on the wall of the Gents. "Did your parents mind you playing truant?" she prodded. "What were they like?"

Spliff was looking bored and was picking bits off a cork drink-mat with his thumbnail. "My mother was a rattlesnake and my father was a warthog, according to *The Herald*. But don't worry, sweetheart, it's a biological impossibility. I checked."

My mother's just like that bloody parrot we used to have, thought Fern. Never says anything when you want it to, and pecks you whenever you get within range. I hope she's watching when I'm on *Missing Link*. She *has* to watch it.

Fern considered phoning her – and then she thought about the indifferent way her mother would say, *oh, it's you*, and she couldn't face it. A postcard. That would do the trick, and it would be there the following morning. Sandra found her a card with a picture of the studios on it, and she thought for a moment. Then she wrote:

> *Watch* Missing Link *tonight when Fern Marshall finds out who her real father is.*

That ought to do it. Sandra said she'd post it for her, which was nice of her.

Fern decided it might be more exciting to find her way back to reception on her own. She left a note on the washstand, and went out into the corridor. In the distance a pale, mousy-haired girl was walking towards her. Fern tried to act unconcerned, and although she smiled briefly she avoided the girl's eyes; she didn't want anyone asking her what she was doing.

She didn't meet anyone famous, and on the way home she started to think about the sort of characters Spliff might have dredged up from her past. Was there anyone she wanted to meet again? Not really, apart from that waiter in Ibiza. Life just happens to me, thought Fern, I never seem to have any control over it. My husband didn't want me, the parrot didn't want me, my mother didn't want me. But *Missing Link* does.

* * *

Jessica sat on the white leather sofa in the studio and waited. What was Spliff going to ask her? If the subject of her parents came up she knew she'd be fighting back the tears. Fifteen months isn't a long time, is it? Not when both of them die within a week of one another. Incidents, anecdotes, character sketches, that's what she was going to need. If she had to do this, she was going to do it well. Her mind drifted back to the time she broke her arm.

There were lots of children playing in the churchyard that day, throwing handfuls of leaves like snowballs. Jessica dodged the wrong way, and collided with a boy; as she fell her arm twisted beneath her and she heard something snap.

Two weeks later, her arm in plaster, she went with her parents to the house of the boy who had done the dastardly deed. She'd never been to the estate before and it was a shock. The vehicles that lined the road were like battered toys, and when the three of them got out of the Mercedes she felt as though a hundred eyes were watching her every move.

"Whad'yer want?" growled the woman who opened the door.

"We feel that you ought to see the consequences of your son's actions," said Jessica's father. "Show her your arm."

Jessica showed the woman her arm.

The woman sneered and said, "What's it got to do with you anyway, grandad?"

The memory stopped there.

The research assistant came over. "There's been a bit of a hitch," she said, glancing off set. "You may as well go back to your dressing room for a while. Would you like another coffee?"

Jessica shook her head and they disentangled her from the radio mike.

"You know your way back all right?"

She nodded.

But it was like a labyrinth down there, and before long she was lost. Corridor after corridor unwound before her, and there didn't seem to be a system; turn the corner from room twenty-four and it was room two hundred and four. She kept walking. Thirty-two, thirty-one, this was more hopeful . . .

She turned another corner and it was back to ninety-five.

A door opened and a woman came out. They walked along the corridor towards one another, and the closer they got the more unsettling the woman's face became. Jessica felt as though she ought to know her, and at the same time she was quite certain she'd never seen her before. The woman smiled nervously and averted her eyes as she passed.

"What the hell are you doing here?" said Spliff, suddenly materialising beside her.

"I got lost."

"We can't have you roaming all over the place. Bloody Prudence. She ought to stop behaving like a coffee machine and do what she's paid to do, keep an eye on you."

"Why? What am I likely to do?"

"We can't have you bumping into other people from the programme."

"That was her, wasn't it? The person I'm linked with. The woman who passed me a moment ago."

He ignored this. "I can't take you back to your dressing room," he said, "I'm busy. Follow the signs for the lift – it says *lift,* with an arrow."

"If I'd seen any signs," said Jessica, "I'd have

followed them. I can manage a four-letter word."

"You surprise me," said Spliff dryly. "Down to the end and turn right. You want the third floor . . . On second thoughts, I'll come with you. Hang on." He disappeared into the room he'd just left, and she heard voices. Then he came out carrying a sheaf of papers and they walked down the corridor together, turned right and entered the lift. He leant across her to push the button, and she recoiled slightly; she really didn't want to touch him.

"I don't bite," said Spliff. "Not on this early an acquaintance, anyway."

They went up in silence to the third floor and got out.

"Down to the end of the corridor and turn left," said Spliff. "I've got great confidence in you now."

"That's more than I have in you," said Jessica.

"Very wise," said Spliff.

Jessica found her room without any difficulty this time, and threw herself down on the sofa. She got out the book she'd brought with her, but she couldn't concentrate, she kept reading the same paragraph over and over again. What was it Spliff knew about her that she didn't know herself?

Three

Elspeth was humming to herself as she sorted out the clothes she would wear the next day. She felt important; she had provided a lot of material for the show – photographs, videos, the address of Jessica's fearsome aunt who lived in Edinburgh.

More than anything, though, she wanted to meet Spliff. She'd had a crush on him ever since she'd seen him arrange to have a sweet little old lady's book published. It brought a real lump to her throat, that electric moment when he said:

"Frances Fortescue, I want you to meet . . . *your publisher*."

The book was total garbage; gratuitous sex and violence in an old people's home. It became a bestseller due to the publicity it got through *Missing Link*. The TV company got a nice cut of the royalties, but Elspeth wasn't to know that.

* * *

Jessica had been told to go and have lunch in the canteen. Prudence went with her, apparently convinced that continuous conversation was the best therapy for stage-fright. They stood in the queue and shuffled forward a few paces at a time.

"I like the avocados, they do a lovely sauce . . . that's Nicholas Creed sitting over there, you know, the newsreader . . ."

Jessica wasn't listening. She'd seen Spliff over the other side of the room, arguing with someone and pushing his salad around the table as though he wished it were light infantry. "Who's that with Spliff?" she asked.

Prudence glanced across the room, and looked wary for a moment. "You know, you saw him in the studio. Clive, the producer. What'll you have, tea or coffee? Or something cold?"

"What are they arguing about?"

"I've no idea," said Prudence, steering Jessica to the opposite side of the room. They sat down and started to eat. Famous faces came and went.

Jessica studied Spliff from a distance. He was undeniably small and tubby, but his movements had a quickness about them, almost a grace. She watched as he stood up and scanned the canteen, looking for someone. Clive said something, Spliff said something back and Clive looked furious.

Spliff sat down again and smiled spitefully.

He had an expressive face, in an economical sort of way. He seemed to be able to go from polite interest to derision without doing very much at all. Perhaps it was the eyes. They were very clear and grey, and rimmed with black lashes that gave them a slightly feminine appearance. The rest of his face was unremarkable, not handsome, not ugly. Black hair, thinning a little at the crown; a dark green shirt that buttoned up to the throat, well-designed and expensive.

A woman with coppery hair extensions went over and said something. Spliff got up, pushed back his chair with some force, and walked off. He slammed the canteen door behind him. The woman shrugged, and sat down opposite Clive. Jessica caught a glimpse of her name label: Patsy.

Prudence watched Spliff's head disappear down the corridor, which was all she could see of him through the little round window in the door. Then she turned to Jessica and said, "Tell me about a family holiday."

"Why? Do you know what Spliff's going to ask me?"

"Not exactly. I don't know the tie-in, you see, the other guest has a different researcher. But describing a holiday would be good practice for you. Tell me about the one in Costa Rica."

"Why that one?"

"I think I saw it on his list," said Prudence confidentially. "I shouldn't say that, but you might not feel quite so nervous if you've got something prepared."

They'd seen electric-blue morpho butterflies the size of dinner plates, armadillos, turtles, flocks of parrots – but she had loved the hummingbirds best of all. They were certainly beautiful, with their fluorescent greens and blues and purples; undeniably delicate, with their long slender beaks and their tiny vibrating wings. But they were little hooligans of birds, confrontational, aggressive, *see you Jimmy!* They'd chase one another all over the garden, pursuing personal vendettas to ridiculous lengths. No one expects a hummingbird to hold a grudge. Appearances can be deceptive.

They were to stay with a Doctor Klein, a friend of her parents. When they arrived at his house in the middle of a thunderstorm he appeared on the veranda, a small man with steel-grey hair. "So," he shouted, making himself heard above the downpour, "this is the little Jessica!" The flowers in his garden dripped and nodded.

"Worth waiting for!" shouted Jessica's father. They went inside.

"Come, now," said Doctor Klein, "you didn't have to wait as long as some. Champagne, I think."

"That would be lovely," said Jessica's mother. "And a Coke or something for Jessica?"

When the drink arrived it came with a little paper mat beneath it, and a napkin to soak up the condensation from the cold glass. Nothing was too much trouble – you want to see turtles laying their eggs in the sand? We go to Tortuguero. Iguanas? Manuel Antonio, and maybe you hear howler monkeys. You like animals, don't you? It is because you are an only child.

And everywhere they went, his camera went too. Jessica at the top of Irazu, looking down into the crater. Jessica holding the lizard she caught in the garden, the stick insect, the bush cricket, the coconut that nearly fell on her head. ("God above, it could have killed her, come away child, we don't want any accidents.") He was just as overprotective as her parents.

"What do you want to do when you grow up?" he asked her.

"Could I do drawing?"

"Yes, yes, you can do art at college. Draw me a picture."

She drew some elephants. He put it in a frame and hung it on the wall in his office, next to several other pictures that looked as though they'd been executed by children. One of the paintings had "Samantha, April 2004" written in one corner.

"Is Samantha your daughter?" asked Jessica.

He smiled. "No. My wife could not have children."

"You've got a wife?" She glanced round her, as though he might have been hiding one on top of the bookshelves or in the fridge.

He patted her on the head. "She died, a long time ago now."

"He sounds like a lonely man," said Prudence, stirring her coffee as though it were liquid gold.

The canteen door opened and Spliff came back in. Heads turned in his direction, and the couple opposite Jessica nudged one another. He looked towards the table he'd occupied with Clive a few minutes before, but Clive had gone and only Patsy remained. Then he saw Jessica and Prudence. He walked over to them, pulled up a chair and sat down.

"Jessica was talking about Costa Rica," said Prudence. "It was really interesting."

"Oh," said Spliff, "don't mind me. Where had you got up to?"

For a moment she had the odd impression that she'd known him for a long time; then she realised that perhaps it was *he* who knew *her*.

"Aaron Klein," she said.

"Oh yes. Did he have any visitors whilst you were out there?"

"Not really . . . well, there was one. Everyone had gone into San José, shopping. Apart from Consuela, that is. The maid. I heard arguing, and it got louder and louder. I crept into the hall to listen, and I caught a glimpse of a girl; she was about twenty I suppose, and she was crying. I heard Consuela say, '*Señor Klein no está aquí.*' "

Spliff looked very interested indeed.

"The woman asked when he would be coming back, and I realised she was American. '*Madre de dios,*' said Consuela, '*No hablo inglés.*' 'I do,' I said,

'I *am* English.' The two women stared at me as though I'd just dropped through the ceiling. The American girl made a sort of strangled sound and ran off down the road, it was weird. Consuela shrugged, tapped her forehead with her finger and laughed. Then she strode back to the kitchen with the clear intention of ironing the sheets to within an inch of their lives."

Spliff laughed, but his eyes had the stillness of someone who was filing information in a very calculated way. What possible relevance could there be in a tearful American girl Jessica had never seen since? She pushed away her empty cup. "We spent the last weekend at Manuel Antonio, on the Pacific coast."

A big man with a ginger moustache suddenly appeared beside them. She recognised him; he was one of the cameramen, and his name was Harry. "Time's getting on," he said.

"Jessica's telling us about Costa Rica," said Spliff. "Grab a chair and listen."

Harry shrugged, and nodded at Jessica to continue.

"Manuel Antonio was the place to see land crabs," Jessica said. "Spectacular things, red, white and blue – a really bright blue. Cerulean."

She glanced at Spliff, wondering whether he knew what cerulean was. He smiled at her, and she had no idea whether he knew or not.

"They would vanish down their burrows when I got too close," she went on, "apart from this one crab, who seemed prepared to attack something a hundred times his own size rather than retreat. He insulted me in semaphore with his pincers, pure white, like the gloves of the traffic police. He was so small compared to me, so determined not to let it make any difference . . ."

"You're sure he was a boy then," said Spliff.

Jessica smiled. "Girls are far more sensible."

"It was a lovely holiday, wasn't it?" said Prudence brightly. "I wish I could go to Costa Rica. Did you ever see Aaron Klein again?"

"Once," said Jessica.

"You make him sound like a nice man."

"He *was* a nice man," said Jessica.

"What constitutes a nice man?" said Spliff unexpectedly.

"Someone who doesn't harm other people."

"What about someone who harms other people unintentionally?"

"Spliff . . ." said Harry. "We really ought . . ."

"Yeah, yeah, yeah," said Spliff, "back to work everyone."

They all got up and trailed out into the corridor.

"Spliff," said Harry, "ever checked a fuel injector? What was the highest pressure reading you got?"

"Thirty."

They launched into an obscure technical discussion that lasted all the way back to the studio.

Four

Harry went back to his camera. Spliff flicked through his notes, and Jessica sipped at her glass of water and waited. The house was on the screen again behind them.

Jessica glanced round the studio, piecing it together. The ceiling was dotted with lights, although most of them were switched off, and the seating rose in a semicircle two-thirds of the way back. The make-up room and wardrobe department had doors opening onto the floor, behind thick black curtains. The set itself was fairly plain. The three walls had a tessellated chain design in silver on a dark grey background, and there were some shallow steps that led up to an exit behind the middle one. In the centre of the floor there was a white leather sofa, a white leather chair and a glass coffee table. On the table there was a carafe of water, some glasses, and a vase of white chrysanthemums. Jessica sat on the sofa, and Spliff sat on the chair.

Behind them, to his left and her right, was a large screen that usually just said *Missing Link – the chain reaction starts here.*

"What do you mean, scrap the birth?" said Spliff suddenly. "We've got it on video." She realised he was talking to the producer through his mike. He smiled at her as though he'd just said what a nice day it was.

If that's the video of my birth I'm glad Clive stopped him, thought Jessica. I wonder where he got hold of it. Elspeth? Elspeth could have copied it without me knowing.

"Let's hear a little bit about your childhood," said Spliff pleasantly. "You lived in a private village, didn't you, security guards, electronic gates, broken glass on top of the walls . . ."

"You make it sound like a prison," said Jessica. "It wasn't. I had a very happy childhood."

"But lonely."

"Not really."

"Tell us a bit about your mother."

Jessica swallowed. "Well . . . she was ill a lot."

"No, no," said Spliff, "what we want is an incident . . . a bit of colour . . . an illustration. I remember the time when . . . that sort of thing. Let's try it again. Tell us a bit about your mother."

Jessica tried not to get rattled and said clearly, "I remember the time we went to an open evening at school and she was taken ill. It was quite funny, really."

"Funny?" He raised an eyebrow. "Go on."

Wrong adjective. She wouldn't make that mistake live. She started to talk about the open evening, but with every sentence a tangled skein of images skittered through her mind. The words were just the shorthand version, slow and clumsy; the real memory ran along underneath, filling in the spaces.

She had trailed round behind her mother and father, apologising for her inattentiveness in class. Only in the art room did she come into her own; her paintings were all over the walls and the art teacher (known as Price the Paint) launched into such a paean of praise that her father embarrassed her dreadfully by saying, "Monet couldn't have done it better."

"And your mother?" said Spliff. "What did your mother have to say about it?"

"I don't remember," said Jessica.

"Don't you?" said Spliff.

My mother never said anything, thought Jessica. Never once did she say that anything I drew was any good. She usually tried to change the subject to something safe like her houseplants, or her latest illness.

"I don't think she said anything," said Jessica.

Jessica's mother grew African violets, cysts, polyps and fibroids. "Oh dear," she said to Price the Paint, "I think I'm going to have a turn."

Jessica's heart sank.

Price the Paint smiled at Jessica; it was faintly conspiratorial, and Jessica was surprised. She'd always assumed that parents and teachers were part of some authoritarian mafia, and she expected to be excluded from it for a good few years yet. "She could lie down in the medical room," said Price the Paint.

Unbeknown to Jessica, two sixth-formers were about to unleash their first-aid expertise on a make-believe casualty, injuries unknown. The casualty was to be the caretaker, and the long gash from his scalp to his chin took a bit longer to execute than anticipated. When the first-aiders arrived at the medical room they found Jessica's mother instead, and they left the door open for the benefit of the small audience outside.

"Hello," said one of the sixth-formers, "my name's Sharon. Can you tell me your name?"

"Mrs Pierce," said Jessica's mother.

"Do you have any pain?" asked Sharon, starting to undo the neck of Jessica's mother's blouse.

"Excuse *me*," said Christine Pierce, removing Sharon's hand.

Sharon and the other girl looked at one another.

"Sorry I'm late," said the caretaker, appearing in the doorway as a road traffic accident.

Christine Pierce took one look, and passed out

for real.

Spliff laughed and Jessica felt pleased, as though she'd pulled a rabbit out of a hat.

"You said you weren't a lonely child," said Spliff. "I think you're lying."

She froze, and her mind went blank.

Spliff threw down his clipboard onto the table. "Oh come on," he said, "you can do better than that."

The cameramen looked at one another. Out of the corner of her eye she could see Clive with a thunderous expression saying something to Prudence.

"You were miserable as sin, weren't you?" said Spliff, "I know *I* was. I was an only child as well."

"I think we'll call a halt there for the moment," said Clive. "Spliff. A word."

"Wanker?" suggested Spliff.

"Things aren't going too well today," said Prudence, "I think Spliff has got a headache or something. And he doesn't like working with Clive. It's a bit hard on poor old Clive, actually, just coming into it for the last one of the series. He's a sweetie really."

"What happened to the previous producer?"

"Simon Tree. His contract ran out."

"Either he resigned or he got the sack," said Jessica, playing a hunch. "Nobody's contract runs out on the penultimate episode."

Prudence looked cornered. "He resigned."

"Why?"

"I don't know."

Jessica could see that she wasn't going to get anything more out of her. She changed the subject. "Do you know him well? Spliff, I mean."

Prudence coloured. "Oh, you know. Yes and no."

* * *

When Fern got back to her flat after her session with Sandra, one of her long-term reflexology clients rang; could she fit her in right then? Fern obliged as she always did; she couldn't afford to turn it down. When the doorbell buzzed she felt a sudden stab of euphoria – this just might be the last time she had to do feet; tomorrow night she might be rich.

"Make sure you watch *Missing Link* tomorrow," said Fern, "I'm on it."

"Oh wow," said Annie, taking off her shoes. "You've got guts."

"Guts?" replied Fern, washing her hands. "Why?"

Annie lay down on the couch. "I've known you for five years Fern," said Annie, "and you've told me some pretty private stuff."

"I didn't tell *them* any of it," said Fern, giggling, "what do you take me for, an idiot?"

"They find things out. Unpleasant things."

Fern sobered straight away. "If I'm thinking what you're thinking, there's no way they'd find out anything about Karl. Not unless you've . . ."

"Fern," said Annie. "I *wouldn't*."

Fern massaged Annie's foot in silence and tried not to remember Karl, but he hovered behind her eyelids in unguarded moments, offering her sweets. Oh yes, Karl had been very friendly. Not her mother's usual type at all.

She'd been fourteen when he first appeared on the scene. He was going to teach her mother to play tennis, and much to Fern's surprise he'd offered to teach her as well. To begin with it was a threesome, and it was really good fun. Then he started offering to take her on her own. Fern's mother was delighted that they were getting on so well; Karl didn't drink and he had a job. He was a bit strange from time to time, but that's insignificant compared to a regular income. He bought Fern a cheap tennis dress, smoothing it over her hips and checking that the zip worked all right.

Then one weekend he offered to stay over with her whilst her mother went away on a course. Fern's mother was thrilled. Fern wasn't so sure. Karl cooked her dinner and gave her some wine. It was the first time she'd drunk any, and it went straight to her head. Then he took her upstairs and raped her.

It sounded such a violent word, rape, because it hadn't been violent at all. It was only later that she had learned to call the act by its real name. She hadn't yet had a boyfriend, and he said it was about time someone taught her what to expect; he was doing her a favour. She didn't know what to say or how to protest. He wasn't holding her down or anything, he was talking quite reasonably as though it was a small but neglected part of her education. The first time he did it was through sheer persuasion from a position of power.

She found it messy and a bit painful, and she wasn't sure what she was meant to get out of it. The grunting was rather unexpected. She didn't tell anyone, but she didn't want it to happen again. The next time he told her that if she didn't do what he wanted, he would tell her mother she'd come on to him. She acquiesced. For the next six months she acquiesced, and then she realised she was pregnant.

She told him. He disappeared, and her mother was really upset about him leaving.

Fern felt it was all her fault. Then, by chance, she bumped into Dermot, one of her mother's ex-boyfriends. He asked her why she was looking so down, and she burst into tears and told him she was in the club. He bought her a bar of chocolate and gave her the address of a posh clinic that did terminations for nothing if they kept the aborted tissue for research. Fern knew he wouldn't say anything to her mother (they weren't speaking any more) so her mother never knew anything about the termination. She thought her daughter went away to stay with a friend for a couple of days – came back with a bit of a temperature, but eventually the fever burnt itself out.

"Television's got no conscience, Fern," said Annie. "Even serial killers have agents these days."

"I don't think it's going to be anything to do with *Karl*," said Fern, "I think it's going to be about my father."

"Don't get too excited," said Annie. "Your mother's choice of men wasn't anything to write home about."

Five

Someone came over and said, "Clive says go and do a trial make-up run." Prudence looked slightly surprised, as though this wasn't normal policy at all, but she took Jessica over to the make-up room.

They sat in front of the mirror, waiting for the make-up artist. Prudence peered at her own reflection. Her face was too long to be really pretty, but her blonde hair had a healthy sheen and her big white teeth had the designer stamp of a good orthodontist. She applied more lipstick and surveyed the result. "I look more like my gran than my mother," she said. "What are your grandparents like?"

"I've no idea," said Jessica. "They all died before I was born."

"Oh, yes of course, silly me," said Prudence. "What a shame."

"Yes," said Jessica, "it was. The only other relative I have is my aunt Maureen."

Jessica's mother seemed to have spent most of her childhood fighting with her sister Maureen. Jessica often wondered whether this reported catalogue of spite had been embellished to promote the advantages of being an only child. Did sisters really steal one another's toys and ritually sacrifice them down the end of the garden on the solstice? It seemed unlikely. Surely siblings were there to share your childhood, stand up for you, compare notes with you in later life?

"I hated my sister," said Prudence. "I don't now of course, we ring each other up all the time. When we were children she told me there was a monster who lived under my bed, and I was terrified of falling asleep for years."

"That's dreadful," said Jessica.

Prudence laughed. "It's normal. Brothers and sisters prepare you for the injustices of the world. Without them, the real world must be a real shock."

"A gradual shock. My parents were so straight with me, you see; I still expect everyone to treat me fairly, tell the truth, listen to what I have to say."

"Oh dear," said Prudence.

"Hi, I'm Louise-Marie," said the make-up artist from behind Jessica, popping up in the mirror like a spring-loaded toy. Her face was painted to doll-like perfection, her straight black hair cut in an immaculate bob. She re-arranged her features into a smile so brief that laughter lines wouldn't be on the agenda for quite a while and said, "The natural look, or something a bit more glamorous?" Although she had a strong French accent, her English was faultless.

"Something a bit more glamorous," said Jessica. Why not? But at the same time she wondered what Louise-Marie could do with hazel eyes that were set a little too closely together and a pasty skin. She leant back in the chair and watched as the woman laid out an assortment of pots and brushes.

Prudence was looking a bit perplexed. "We don't usually have a trial make-up run," she said.

"Spliff will have his reasons," said Louise-Marie.

"How old is he?" Jessica asked.

"Thirty," said Prudence.

"And the rest," said Louise-Marie.

"It says thirty on the biography sheet," said Prudence.

"He wrote that himself," said Louise-Marie. "It's all lies."

"He wouldn't do that," said Prudence.

Louise-Marie allowed herself a tight little laugh. "Spliff will do anything if he feels like it. He's amoral. He doesn't play by any rules except his own."

"Then he's not amoral, is he?" said Prudence. "Not if he's got his own rules."

"You don't like him, do you?" Jessica said to Louise-Marie.

"Like isn't really a word you use about Spliff," said Louise-Marie.

"*I* like him," said Prudence.

Louise-Marie smeared foundation over

Jessica's face. "He's going to go too far one of these days, Prudence, he gets a buzz out of . . ."

"Er . . ." Prudence glanced meaningfully at Jessica.

"*Pardon*," said Louise-Marie to Jessica. "I didn't mean to put you off. I expect you'll be one of the lucky ones with a Leonardo in the loft."

Spliff suddenly appeared in the doorway. Prudence coloured slightly, and Louise-Marie dropped a tub of cleanser. A couple of splashes of yellow hit the mirror, and the air seemed to thicken like custard. Louise-Marie reached across for a tissue and wiped it up.

Spliff pointed to the clock, and looked questioningly at the French girl.

"Two minutes?" said the make-up artist.

"Splendid, darling," said Spliff, impersonating Clive to perfection. He went over to Louise-Marie and brushed her shoulder with the tips of his fingers, the way Clive would sometimes do when he was talking to someone. Unthinkingly fastidious, as though he was absent-mindedly dusting them.

Louise-Marie smiled, although it was apparent she didn't want to, she just couldn't help herself. She dipped a brush in some eyeliner, and as she lifted her arm to apply it Spliff caught hold of her wrist. He opened her fingers, quite slowly, one by one, and took hold of the brush. "Don't overdo it," he said softly, "we want her looking natural."

"She said she wanted something a bit more

glamorous."

"She doesn't need it," replied Spliff.

"It *is* waterproof," said Louise-Marie sharply. She had a hard face that seemed to change expression geometrically, like a Cubist painting made flesh.

Spliff's eyes narrowed fractionally. "What have you been saying?"

"Only what a delightful person you are to work with."

"I'm not when people piss me about," said Spliff.

"I know," said the French girl.

Jessica was watching them all in the mirror. Spliff glanced in her direction, and their eyes met fleetingly. "Two minutes then," he said, "and no eye shadow, no eyeliner, no mascara, and no blusher. You'd better powder her nose, though."

The atmosphere was a lot better this time. They rattled through a few straightforward questions about Jessica's mother, and a photograph of Christine Pierce appeared on the big screen behind them. The computer image looked down on them, larger than life, and with an expression of faint distaste. The baby-blue eyes were accentuated with just the right amount of eye-shadow, and the baby-blonde hair undulated like a Van Gogh cornfield. It must have been taken about ten years previously. Spliff turned to look at the screen. "A beautiful woman, even in old age. Dyed her hair?"

"Yes."

"Electrolysis?"

"What?"

"Hair removal. Upper lip, usually. Facelift?"

"I don't think so," said Jessica faintly.

He flipped over a page on his clipboard. "I think it would be fair to say that you take after your father when it comes to looks?"

"Yes." And the lack of make-up only made it all the more obvious.

"Before we move on to him, just one last question Jessica. When was your mother born?"

Jessica hesitated. "I don't know exactly . . ."

"You've never seen her birth certificate?"

"No."

"Well, who dealt with all the funeral arrangements then?"

"My aunt Maureen," said Jessica. "She did everything."

"Everything?"

"Yes," said Jessica, annoyed. "Everything. I was too upset. That's reasonable, isn't it?"

Spliff looked at his notes, and ran his finger along something. "In that case," he said, "if you've never seen your mother's birth certificate, your mother might not have been who she said she was at all . . ." He turned to the producer. "Stop that bit there then, Clive?"

Clive raised his thumb.

"What do you mean," said Jessica, "she might

not have been who she said she was?"

"Don't worry about it," said Spliff, "we always throw in a few red herrings."

"What do you mean?"

"We keep the viewers guessing . . . make them think, ah, that's what it's going to be about. Then we surprise them with something else entirely."

He scribbled something on one of his sheets of paper, thought for a moment, then glanced up at her. Jessica suddenly felt that he knew more about her than she did herself; that he knew not only her history but her thoughts, her aspirations, her fantasies. It was almost indecent. His eyes travelled very slowly across her face like fingertips familiar with the terrain. It felt like a seduction as well as an invasion – she had his entire attention and she felt distinctive, singular, special, as though she'd suddenly turned three-dimensional and technicoloured and – yes, *sexy*. She shivered.

"We'll just do your father," said Spliff, "then we'll take a break. After that we'll do your friend Elspeth, then we'll touch on boyfriends . . ."

Jessica stiffened.

He smiled. "We did sheep for one young lad."

"What?"

"Sheep. Joke, Jessica. Lighten up. This is meant to be fun."

"Anyone for coffee?" said Prudence brightly.

"For once Priscilla," said Spliff, "you got it right. Jessica?"

Jessica nodded. Prudence looked cut to the quick at being called Priscilla, and went off to get the coffee.

"You'll be fine," said Spliff, "you're tougher than you think. You can handle it."

Handle what? It was almost a threat, and she felt a faint frisson of danger. Their eyes met again, and held. She tried to read his face. He smiled very slightly, as though he knew exactly what she was doing and he was just letting her do it. After a moment what she was doing with her eyes felt as improper as what he'd done to her, and she glanced away. She fought back another shiver. How could this rather unpleasant man turn himself into someone so charismatic, by the simple expedient of flattering her and threatening her at the same time? One of the rabble that made it, low life to high life, lager to champagne. Was this how he'd done it, with tricks and treats? Did he just have the knack of making you feel truly unique, the sexiest compliment of all?

"They're putting you up in the Royal tonight?" he said.

"Yes."

"See you in the bar, then."

"All right," said Jessica, suddenly aghast at herself for replying at all, let alone in the affirmative.

Prudence appeared with the coffee.

"It's a pretty naff bar," said Spliff, "sort of modernised modern. The beer's good though, which is why we all go there for a pint and a bite to eat after work. OK. Page seven."

Prudence looked from one face to the other.

"Prudence," said Spliff.

Prudence looked miserable and walked away.

There was a faint crackle, and then a couple of the lights blew out. Spliff threw down the clipboard and stood up. "If that's bloody Andy again," he shouted, "I'll fucking well hang him by his lighting flex from the gantry."

"Get stuffed," came a voice from behind the curtains.

Nobody laughed. They all looked at Spliff. "Two blow-jobs in two days," said Spliff. "Nice one, Andy."

"Children," said Clive, "the lights don't matter at the moment, let's just get on with it."

"Just give me a minute then," said Spliff, "whilst I electrocute the chiromaniac."

"Spliff," said Clive, "have a bit of consideration for Jessica, will you? I'm sure she's got better things to do than to listen to you slagging off members of the crew."

"She probably hasn't even heard half the words you use," said Harry, "give her a break, Spliff."

"What's a chiromaniac?" said Jessica.

"A wanker," said Spliff.

Clive threw down his clipboard.

"I'm not a nun," said Jessica, more annoyed at Clive's attitude towards her than she was at Spliff's vocabulary. "I am aware of other habits apart from the ankle-length variety."

Spliff laughed.

Jessica felt the back of her neck prickle. It was as though the two of them suddenly had their backs to the wall, growling and spitting at the opposition, unexpected allies. She was part of a skirmish she didn't understand, there were undercurrents here; she was siding with Spliff of all people – or had he just co-opted her without her consent?

"Knock it off, Spliff," said Harry. "Clive's only trying to get the job done."

Six

"Edward Pierce," said Spliff, glancing behind him. A photograph of a white-haired man appeared on the screen, a delta of laughter lines around the close-set hazel eyes. Jessica suddenly felt on the verge of tears.

Spliff said, "Daddy's girl?"

She recovered herself, and they talked about the churchyard incident and Costa Rica for a couple of minutes.

"What do you know about his childhood?" asked Spliff.

She'd been expecting it, racking her brains to remember something, *anything* she could talk about. There wasn't a lot. "He collected things," she said. "He was an only child as well."

"There are quite a lot of us, aren't there?" remarked Spliff.

The producer looked up sharply. Once again Jessica had the baffling impression that she and Spliff were on the same side about something that totally eluded her.

"What did he collect?" asked Spliff.

"Oh," said Jessica, "I don't know. Books, glass bottles, shards of pottery. He wanted to study history, but his parents had different ideas."

She was back in the conservatory, eating grapes and watching her father fiddling with the stem of his wineglass as he talked. Six months later he would be dead.

"There wasn't anyone I knew who understood how I felt about antiques," her father was saying, "no one. Don't be diverted from what you really want to do, Jessica. If you want to be a painter, go for it, whatever your mother says."

"She hasn't said anything about me going to art school."

"No," he said, "I don't suppose she has."

It was the nearest he'd ever come to criticising Jessica's mother. What else might he have told me, Jessica wondered, if he'd lived longer? Is that another thing I've missed out on, the opportunity to speak to my parents as another adult, to learn things they couldn't tell me when I was a child?

"I did what my parents wanted," said Jessica's father. "I studied chemistry. But in the end I went into antiques after all."

"In the end he went into antiques . . ." said Spliff. "In the end. What we're really interested in is what Edward Pierce did in between getting a first in chemistry and buying an antiques business. A period spanning a considerable number of years."

"I thought he went straight into antiques after college," said Jessica, "doing restoration stuff. You need chemistry for that."

Spliff smiled. "It may surprise you to know," he said, "that he did in fact work for . . . blah, blah, blah . . . fairly boring, don't get edgy. We save that for when we go out live. What we're really focusing on is the people he knew whilst he worked there. Any old friends who came to visit?"

"Only Doctor Klein."

"Aaron Klein. Yes. We'll come back to him later as well. Nobody else, though?"

"No. Only other antique people." She wished she hadn't said it the moment the words were out, and she knew immediately that her face had given it away. He'd been drawing attention to her parents' age all the way through. They'd been good parents. Surely that was more important?

"Damn," said Spliff, "I wish you'd said that tomorrow."

"No chance," said Jessica.

"We'll see," said Spliff. "I'm very persuasive."

"Really," she said.

He wrote something down. "Did your father

ever mention someone called Eveline?"

"I don't think so."

"Suzannah?"

"No."

"Laura?"

"No."

"Svetlana?"

"Svetlana?"

"Let's take a break there," said Spliff.

Everyone drifted over to the cold drinks machine in little groups. Prudence was nowhere to be seen. Jessica got herself a mineral water, and sat down on one of the steps that led up to the audience seating. She heard Louise-Marie talking to someone behind the staging.

"I don't know why any of them agree to it," said the make-up artist. "I really don't."

"It's a sort of deification," said a man's voice.

"Oh come off it, Clive," said Louise-Marie. "You can take this intellectualising of crap television too far."

"Tell me any other way your average pleb is going to get himself recognised in every shop down the high street," said Clive. "Fame. A fleeting sense of self-worth. People will sell their souls for that."

"What's the tie-in on this one?" asked Louise-Marie.

Clive said something inaudible.

There was a slight pause. "He's not a very happy bunny," said Louise-Marie.

"Tough," said Clive.

"He doesn't like you."

"I don't like him."

"He makes this show," said Louise-Marie. "They won't get rid of him, whatever he does."

There was another pause. Then Clive said, "Did the two of you . . . did you ever . . ."

"Hasn't everyone?" said Louise-Marie.

"I've no idea," said Clive, "I'm the new boy here, remember? I haven't slept with him, if that's what you're thinking."

Louise-Marie laughed. "He's straight."

"Oh," said Clive. "Any good?"

"That would be telling," said Louise-Marie. "What do you think of the main guest? Face like a Cornish pasty?"

"Sweetie," said Clive, "that was dreadfully unkind."

Jessica got up and walked away.

She found Prudence in the Ladies, looking wretched. She put her arm round her and gave her a tissue. "I expect you've guessed," sniffed Prudence. "I've got a bit of a thing about Spliff. I think I'm in love with him."

"I'm sure you're not," said Jessica.

"Yes I am. I slept with him."

Jessica had an overpowering urge to laugh. Instead she patted Prudence on the shoulder and said, "You shouldn't dwell on it."

Prudence just looked at her.

Jessica gave up and went outside.

Spliff was sitting on the step. "Prudence upset?" he said.

"You could say that."

"Silly cow," said Spliff, "I told her it was just a one-night stand."

"She really cares about you," said Jessica, nettled. "You play with people, don't you? You like the power."

"Mm hm," said Spliff unexpectedly.

"And you think it's all right to treat people like entries in your CV?"

"My God, it'd be one hell of a long CV."

Jessica realised she was clenching her fists.

"That's got you narked, hasn't it?" he said. He was watching her closely. "Prudence needs to grow up a bit; sleeping with her was my contribution to a worthy cause."

His arrogance and dismissiveness hung unspoken between them; her fury wouldn't. "You *are* a bastard, aren't you," she said.

He laughed, and stood up.

She started to walk away.

"No, no," said Spliff, "that was excellent. I needed to know how you'd come across if you were *really* angry."

She turned round and glared at him. He grinned disarmingly. "Go on, go and tell Prudence I'll talk to her." Now he sounded kind, concerned, a decent caring bloke. It also sounded like he was offering *her* the concession, not Prudence, and on top of that she couldn't help feeling annoyed that he just expected her to do as he instructed.

"Well, I can't go in there, can I?" he said, as though she'd voiced it.

"I really don't know how to take you," said Jessica.

"Most positions are fully acceptable," said Spliff.

Jessica turned on her heel and went back into the Ladies. "Spliff wants to see you," she said. "He's outside. I really don't know what you see in the man."

When they reconvened Prudence looked a lot more cheerful.

"OK," said Clive, glancing at the clock, "we've got a lot to get through."

Spliff turned to a new page. Jessica watched him as his eyes flicked down it; then he looked up at her. "OK?"

"Ready for anything."

"An admirable position to be in," said Spliff.

She couldn't help it. She laughed.

"We're devoting some time to Elspeth," said Spliff, "because her parents were friends of your parents, and you've known each other most of your lives."

"Are you going to have her on the

programme?"

"I think so," said Spliff. "I'll need to see how she comes across tomorrow."

"Oh, Elspeth always comes across," said Jessica.

"I'm the one who makes the jokes," said Spliff. "Watch it."

Jessica felt pleased with herself, although it would have been nicer if he'd been more irritated about it. Then she felt annoyed with herself for caring.

Spliff smiled. "Do you remember the time you all spent a week together in a cottage in France?"

There had been a picnic on the beach. Elspeth and Jessica decided to creep up on the adults, and they wriggled along the sand on their stomachs and hid behind the windbreak. Elspeth's father and Jessica's mother were nowhere to be seen, and Jessica's father was rubbing suntan oil into Zoë's shoulders. Zoë was a lot younger than Jessica's mother, and she wore very skimpy bikinis.

"Bit to the right, Edward," said Elspeth's mother.

"How far?" said Jessica's father.

"As far as you like."

Edward laughed.

"You never used to be so circumspect," said Zoë.

"That was a long time ago."

"You can't blame a girl for trying," said Zoë.

"Girl?" hissed Elspeth. "The woman's mad."

"I think your mother's nice," said Jessica.

"Oh, for God's sake," whispered Elspeth. "The woman's a tart."

"Do my legs," said Zoë.

There was a little gurgling sound as Jessica's father upended the suntan oil.

"Whose idea was Jessica?" asked Zoë. "Yours or Christine's?"

"Mine."

"She wasn't as happy with the outcome, was she?"

"God knows why," said Edward. "Jessica's perfect."

"You *know* why," said Zoë. There was a pause.

A wasp buzzed round Jessica's head. "I don't think we ought to be listening to this," she said.

"Why not?"

"We just shouldn't."

"I don't see why not. My mother picks up the extension sometimes and listens to my conversations. She reads my diary, so I put things in it especially to annoy her. I said we played truant last month."

"You *what*?" said Jessica, forgetting herself.

Jessica's father and Elspeth's mother rolled apart. "Hello girls," said Edward, "have a nice walk?"

"Lovely," said Elspeth.

Seven

"Was your mother very self-conscious about her age?" asked Spliff.

"I suppose she was," said Jessica.

"Did you worry about it?"

"How do you mean?"

"Did you worry about it," said Spliff shortly. "It's a perfectly straightforward question."

"I used to wonder who would look after me if they both died."

Prudence bustled over with a piece of paper. Spliff glanced at it, glanced at Clive, got up and walked towards the heavy curtains that surrounded the set.

"Where's he going?" asked Jessica.

"To make a phone call," said Prudence, "something to do with the other guest."

"What's she like?"

"How do you know it's a she?"

"Aha," said Jessica, "I'd make a good research

assistant myself."

"Don't tell Spliff," said Prudence, mortified, "he'll think I've been saying things I shouldn't." She sat down on the sofa next to Jessica.

"Why don't you tell me what happened between the two of you?" said Jessica. The best defence against Spliff might be to know something about him in return.

"Well," said Prudence, "it was all a bit . . . strange, really. We'd just finished recording that episode about the blind woman in the wheelchair. Spliff seemed . . . I don't know, touchy, out of sorts. I'd fancied him for ages. I didn't to start with – nobody does, he sort of grows on you. He can be awfully nice sometimes, really thoughtful, and he does loads of charity work." She fiddled with the thin gold chain round her neck. "Someone asked him if he was going to the bar, and he said no, he intended to go somewhere he could get really blasted. 'Sounds like fun' I said, or something like that. He just looked at me, you know the way he does, you feel there's no point saying anything because he knows it all already. 'So you think you can keep up?' he said."

"Back in a minute," said Clive, to no one in particular.

"We went to some really seedy place where he knew everyone and I didn't know a soul," said Prudence. "He got pretty drunk. Then someone came over and accused him of selling out. He got angry. He said he'd never envisaged doing anything as . . . oh, I shouldn't be saying this."

"No," said Jessica, "I know. Go on."

They grinned at one another, female conspirators.

"He said *Missing Link* was the absolute pits, it was the epitome of everything that was wrong with society. Then this bloke said he thought Spliff epitomised the lowest common denominator pretty well himself, and Spliff just went bonkers, lashed out, you know? Someone came over and separated them. I think he was getting the worst of it, so it's probably just as well. We got a taxi back to his place, and I sort of dabbed his cuts and bruises and made him some coffee. He sobered up a bit, apologised, got out some weed and rolled a joint. I asked him what had upset him so much about the day's recording. 'Old people,' he said. I tried to get him to elaborate, but he wouldn't. We just sat there for ages, getting stoned, listening to Mahler."

"Mahler?"

"I know," said Prudence, "you wouldn't think it, would you? When he gets interviewed he always says real music started with The Bloodsuckers."

"What's his flat like?"

"A mess. Not dirty, just untidy. Books everywhere, old ones, new ones, about everything under the sun. Bits of machinery, DVDs, papers, magazines. The most beautiful collection of lead crystal glassware. A series of framed Escher prints, a genuine Gwen John watercolour. A full-sized tyrannosaurus head in the loo, above where you sit. Weird."

Jessica was becoming ever more curious. "What happened next?"

"It got to about three o'clock," said Prudence, "he suddenly said, 'Do you want me to call a taxi . . . or would you rather I didn't?' I said I'd stay. Then we went to bed." A faraway look came into her eyes.

The crew drifted back and Spliff returned, looking grim. "Off," he said to Prudence. Prudence made herself scarce. "Where were we?" said Spliff, leafing through his papers.

"Elspeth," said Jessica.

"Oh yes." He folded over the page, leant back in his chair and looked at her. She could see immediately that he knew exactly what Prudence had been telling her. "I got the dinosaur from a friend in props," he said casually. "Fabulous thing. Very lifelike."

Jessica laughed. "How can you tell if it's lifelike when no one's ever seen a live one?"

"I have a good imagination," said Spliff, "or didn't Prudence get that far? Did you know that an adult tyrannosaurus weighed five point seven tons?"

"Male or female?" said Jessica, determined to be equally cool. "And which species?"

He looked amused. "Male; *rex*. It's quite impressive. Ask anyone. They've all seen it. Louise-Marie, Patsy, Sandra . . ."

"A seminal experience, no doubt," said Jessica.

His gaze sharpened; it was as though he hadn't had her properly in focus before. He smiled rather thoughtfully and said, "More like an acquired taste."

"Not immediately appetising and rarely satisfying?"

He seemed surprised. "Prudence didn't say that, did she?"

"Can we get a move on?" said Clive.

"You said you had a visit from Aaron Klein," said Spliff. "How old were you?"

"Oh – twelve, thirteen."

"Tell us about it."

Aaron Klein brought her a present. It was a carved wooden box, and inside the box was a complete set of watercolours – not children's paints but the real thing, alizarin crimson, rose madder, Prussian blue, purple lake . . . He showed her how to stretch the paper, how to put on a wash; he taught her the rules of perspective and a bit of colour theory, and it all made perfect sense to her because she'd realised most of it anyway.

She said goodbye to him at the airport. He patted her on the head and said, "You are one of my children. I am proud."

"What do you think he meant?" asked Spliff.

"I know what he meant," said Jessica. "He delivered me. You've seen the video."

Spliff turned the page. "You did adequately but unremarkably at school – an underachiever. You got a scholarship to art school on the basis of your portfolio." He signalled to Clive and said, "Thirty seconds there."

Clive nodded.

"What did your mother say?"

It came out like a reflex action. " 'Well there's one thing that's certain, she didn't get all that artistic nonsense from me.' "

"Do you enjoy art school?"

She talked about her work, the tutors, her flatmates.

"Boyfriends?" asked Spliff.

"No one serious."

"I thought you got engaged to . . ." he glanced at his notes, "Robert Sinclair . . ."

"We broke it off three days later," said Jessica. "I wouldn't call that serious."

"What was the matter with him?" said Spliff.

She laughed. "Nothing. He just . . . I don't know . . ."

"Didn't turn you on?"

"I'm not a light bulb," said Jessica. "Life's a bit more complicated than that."

"No it isn't," said Spliff, "we just like to think it is." He turned over another page. "Going to college is a time when people frequently look at their families in a new light. Did you?"

"Not really," said Jessica.

"Come on," said Spliff, "you must have started to ask a few questions."

"No."

"Nothing out of place with the histories your parents gave you, nothing odd anywhere?"

"No," said Jessica, suddenly feeling as though the ground was dropping away.

"Nothing at all?"

"No."

"Skip the next bit," said Spliff. "I want to go to page twenty-three."

Jessica felt numb. She realised he was watching her.

"This particular programme . . . it's important to me," he said.

"Why?"

He gave her an old-fashioned look. No, thought Jessica, there's no way he'd answer that one, is there? Might give the game away. I'm beginning to think there really *is* something fundamental I don't know about my own background. "Has anyone ever pulled out?" she asked.

"No."

"Nobody at all?"

"Well . . . there was a town planner who feigned a heart attack. We've got a resident doctor now. You didn't read the small print, did you?"

"Not until later." She felt like a complete idiot.

"Nobody does," said Spliff. "That's why it's

worded like that."

"Supposing I really did break a leg . . ."

"Then you'd appear on *Missing Link* in plaster," said Spliff. "Jessica . . . I meant it when I said this one's important. Not just for you. For a lot of people."

She stared at him. "There's something in my life that's absolutely critical to you, isn't there? And I've no idea what it is. No idea at all."

"I'm not going to ask you to trust me," said Spliff. "That would be ridiculous, with my reputation. But stick with it. Can you?"

He's telling me he needs me, thought Jessica. Why? Is it just a ploy to keep me sweet? He's a much cleverer man than I'd expected, and now I'm consumed with even more curiosity than before, and he knows it. She heard herself say, "I have to stick with it, don't I?"

Eight

After Annie put on her sensible shoes and left, Fern poured herself a stiff drink. There were the remains of a curry in the fridge, but she didn't feel like heating them up. She turned on the television, and channel-hopped for a while. Nothing held her attention until she came across Spliff, doing a trailer for the programme the following day.

"Is it going to be heaven or hell for our guests this week?" said the familiar burnt-sugar voice and she felt a sudden thrill of connection. He was talking about *her. Her,* Fern Marshall. He smiled at the camera, and suddenly he was a small boy plotting something vile but hysterically funny. "Will there be tears? Will there be laughter? You'll only find out if you join me tomorrow evening at nine for *Missing Link* . . . the chain reaction starts here, folks. And tomorrow night we could get meltdown, believe me. Make sure you're around for the fallout." There followed a series of quick clips of previous guests in various states of emotional turmoil, from euphoria to blind rage. Fern switched off the television. She had resolutely refused to look at the dark side of the programme up until now, she'd been picturing that electric moment when Spliff would say, "Fern Marshall, I'd like you to meet . . . your father." He'd be a smiley man with silvery hair and he'd tell her that he hadn't known about her until now (that sort of thing happened all the time on television) and he was over the moon about it. He'd be rich and funny and kind, and her life would never be the same again.

But supposing it wasn't her father. Supposing Spliff had got hold of Derek or Alan or Slogger or . . . *Max*.

She'd been ten, eleven maybe. She'd been home alone, her mother had been out somewhere. When the doorbell rang she did what she always did; switched off the lights and kept quiet. The doorbell rang for a long time; it sounded as though someone was leaning on it. Then the blows started, one after the other, equally spaced but increasing in ferocity.

"I know you're in there, you gin-sodden cow, open up!"

Fern had taken against Max the moment he'd asked her to call him daddy. She'd complied (reluctantly) because Max had a sophisticated line in threats; "Do what I say or I'll kick your head in." He had short bronze hair with an almost metallic sheen, and popping-out eyes. A facial tic that wasn't a tic – a half-smile at the end of every sentence, daring you to contradict him. He had never actually hit Fern really hard, but he liked making her cry by saying he was going to. Fern had been ecstatic when her mother had announced that Max was leaving; she'd helped move all his stuff into the hall outside and she'd put a dead rat in one of his boots for good measure. She sat there hardly daring to breathe as the blows got heavier. Nobody would interfere, nobody ever did. There had been a gunshot one night from the flat downstairs, and people were always passing out on the landing or yelling at one another.

"I'm warning you!" shouted Max. "I've got a chainsaw in the van, and I'll use it!"

Fern wriggled under the sofa. It felt safe under there, despite the dust and the empty bottles and the mouse droppings.

A sound of splintering wood told her that the door had given way. She heard Max's footsteps, heard him go into the bedroom, the kitchen, the bathroom. Then he entered the sitting room and switched on the light. She held her breath. After a moment or two he said, "Fucking bitch," and went out again. She heard breaking glass in the kitchen, and the glass carried on breaking for a long time. The parrot started screaming *"fuck off, fuck off,"* and then it went quiet.

When she was absolutely certain that Max had gone, Fern crawled out from her hiding place and went into the kitchen. The parrot eyed her balefully from the top of a set of shelves. Max had smashed everything, even its cage, which took some doing. Glass scrunched underfoot, tomato ketchup was running down the walls and the toaster lay on its side, its wire innards spilling out like intestines. All the tea towels had been shredded with a kitchen knife, a cupboard had been wrenched off the wall and the work surface was splattered with blackcurrant jam.

Fern climbed up on a chair until she was level with the parrot. "Come on," she said, "it's OK now."

"Fuck off," said the parrot, and pecked her.

Fern left it where it was and found some plastic sacks and a dustpan and brush and started to clear up. She was halfway through it when her mother came back.

"What the hell's been going on?" demanded her mother, putting a hand on the work surface to steady herself and withdrawing it rather hastily.

"Max," said Fern.

"Why didn't you stop him?" said her mother, wiping her hand on her skirt.

Fern gaped at her.

"What did you do, skulk under the settee whilst he wrecked the place?"

Fern bit her lip.

"You're *useless*, Fern. He wouldn't have done it if he'd known you were here."

She'd fouled up again.

Her mother hadn't always blamed her for everything that went wrong; it just became an increasing trend as Fern got older. When she'd been small they'd lived in France. She remembered the sunshine and the chocolate croissants and the pistachio ice cream but precious little else, which was a pity as she suspected she'd been reasonably happy then. It was when they moved back to England that it clouded over and the ice cream dried up.

Her mother hadn't been able to find a job for a long time, and they'd moved around a lot. The flats got smaller and smaller until Fern was sleeping on the sofa and her mother preferred gin to breakfast. There wasn't much in the way of conversation, and Fern spent most of her life watching TV. She bunked off school; she couldn't see the point. Her mother had had an education and where had it got her? Nowhere. Fern lived in a pixellated world of limousines and swimming pools, and waited for her knight in shining armour.

He'd eventually materialised in the guise of a muscular Aussie builder called Charlie. They tried for a baby, and Charlie started buying sections of model railway track and tiny tip-up trucks in preparation. "Supposing it's a girl?" said Fern.

Charlie looked slightly worried. But as the months lengthened into years and nothing happened the purchases grew fewer and further between, and Charlie seemed to lose interest. He went to Australia for a long holiday to visit his folks, and he didn't come back.

Fern wasn't unduly surprised. It was what she expected from life by now. There had been a few boyfriends after that, but they only really wanted sex. It had taken Fern a long time to learn to enjoy the process, but she had in the end, thanks to one of her client's husbands.

Oh my God, thought Fern, supposing Spliff's got hold of Rodney?

Rodney had bumped into Fern at the supermarket one day, when they'd both grabbed the same butternut squash from different ends. Somehow or other they'd ended up back at her flat, and as usual she wasn't surprised when she realised that he wanted a screw, not a soup recipe. But Rodney was different. Rodney's ego wouldn't let Fern just lay there; ten years after Karl's instruction course she finally found out what all the fuss was about, and the affair lasted until Rodney moved on to his wife's chiropractor. After that there was Bill and Andrew and Mario, and Fern learnt about suspenders and sex aids and spaghetti. She knew how to have a good time now, but she was still waiting for Mr Right. Maybe he'd be watching tomorrow night.

She finished her vodka and Coke and poured another. She'd been teetotal until she was thirty; her one experience of wine with Karl had been like a short sharp course of aversion therapy, and her mother's dipso behaviour had only reinforced the antipathy. Then Rodney had spiked her orange juice with vodka one day, not too much, just enough to get her merry, and after she'd stopped hitting him with a pillow she realised she'd actually enjoyed herself. Bill got her onto lager and Mario introduced her to Tia Maria, but she never drank wine again. Just the smell of it made her feel queasy.

She wondered how things would have turned out if she'd had a brother or a sister, a co-victim, someone to share the blame. A sister would have been nice. Her mother had been part of a big family, but none of them spoke to her any more. Fern remembered her mother shouting down the phone at various relatives at two in the morning, berating them for things they'd done twenty years earlier or warning them darkly about her latest conspiracy theory. Then she usually became incoherent or abusive and slammed down the handset. One by one the aunts and uncles moved house and went ex-directory, until there were no more phone calls and no more Christmas cards. Fern and her mother became a duo, yoked together by genes, reluctant fellow-travellers down the cul-de-sac of life.

Nine

Jessica got up to stretch her legs. Everyone else relaxed and milled about, and she spotted Prudence's notes on the steps. No clues there, it was written in shorthand and full of acronyms. A sheet of paper fell out. It was Spliff's biography; trust Prudence. She glanced round, and then started to read.

"Spliff," she read, "was born Arthur Whitney on the seventh of April, 1990, in Norwich. He was an only child. Both his parents died before he was seventeen. After a spell as a trucker he landed the part of the football hooligan Jimmy Crushit in *Balls,* and went on to present *The Red Card Game* and *Missing Link.*"

His hobbies were listed as football, drinking, and Classic-Vampire-Scratch. He was quoted as saying that The Bloodsuckers were the next best thing to fellatio, and that the goalkeeper Wittgenstein was the greatest love of his life. There was no mention of Mahler or Escher. She put the sheet of paper back inside Prudence's notes.

"Did you get some coffee?" asked Clive from behind her.

She turned round. "I didn't want any." Close up he seemed rather pleasant; tasteful, neat. "Tell me," said Jessica, "how did Spliff get the part of Jimmy Crushit?"

"He was a member of a drama club at college. Melanie Oaks spotted him." He picked a wisp of fluff off her T-shirt, then he dusted the offending spot with the tips of his fingers exactly the way Spliff had done, when he was impersonating him in the make-up room.

Jessica fought back the urge to laugh and said, "College? I didn't know he went to college. What did he do there?"

"Very little, in all probability," said Clive.

"What subject, though?" Various possibilities flitted through her mind. Sports studies . . . car maintenance . . . bricklaying . . .

"Philosophy."

"Philosophy?"

"Socrates and Wittgenstein and that lot. What else can you do with a philosophy degree other than present a chat show?"

She smiled.

"Time and tide and all that," said Clive. "Back to work."

Jessica went back to the sofa and sat down.

"We've just got the unpleasant bit to do, and then we can call it a day," said Spliff.

"More unpleasant than it's been already?"

"I meant the funeral. It hasn't been that bad, has it?"

"How would you feel," said Jessica, "in my position?"

"I've never tried your position," said Spliff instantly. "Good one, is it?"

She didn't laugh.

"Sorry," said Spliff, although it was quite apparent he wasn't. She really didn't know what to think of him now, none of the things she'd found out about him seemed to fit together.

Clive signalled to him to get on with it.

"Fifteen months ago," said Spliff, "your father died of cancer. Then your mother died of a heart attack five days later."

His voice sounded perfectly normal, but something unexpected flickered across his face and Jessica thought, *that's it*. That's our link, the thing we have in common, the thing that's crucial to the programme. His own parents were dead by the time he was seventeen; I need to find out more.

"A double funeral," said Spliff, "arranged by your aunt Maureen. How did she offer to do it?"

"She didn't offer," said Jessica. "She just did it."

"And you were happy about that? Didn't you want to go through their things yourself?"

"There were no problems with the will or anything, it was all quite straightforward."

"They left everything to you."

"Yes."

"Nobody contested anything?"

"No."

"Fine," said Spliff, "thirty seconds there."

Clive gave him the thumbs up.

"Was it a big funeral?"

"Fairly."

"Antique people, mainly?"

She smiled. "Mainly."

"Eveline," said Spliff. "Was there an Eveline there?"

"Not that I know of," said Jessica.

Who was this Eveline?

"I think we can leave it there for tonight," said Spliff.

Everyone began to pack up. Prudence came over, trying to look nonchalant, her ridiculously healthy hair swinging from side to side. Jessica could see that she'd re-done her make-up and she could smell the Christian Dior perfume and the toothpaste. "Down the bar, then?" she said.

Spliff said something non-committal. Prudence brightened, interpreting it as "yes". A couple of the cameramen swept her away in passing, singing an obscene version of *Ten Green Bottles*.

"You owe me a drink," said Patsy, ruffling Spliff's hair in passing and tossing her copper-coloured hair extensions over one shoulder. They must have cost a fortune; some of them were intertwined with threads of pewter.

"Are you coming Jessica?" asked another woman she'd only seen from a distance. She was a strikingly beautiful redhead, with perfect bone structure and grey-green eyes. Jessica looked at Spliff. She felt at a loss, she didn't know what she was supposed to do or who she was supposed to go with.

"Give us a minute Sandra," said Spliff, not looking up from his paperwork. "I just want to go over a couple of things with Jessica."

The studio emptied. Jessica felt superfluous, her confidence had ebbed away, she wanted to go home.

Spliff looked up and glanced round. "Hungry?"

"I suppose I am. Yes."

He put away his pen, got up and picked up his jacket. It didn't look as though he needed to go over anything with her after all. Jessica found her coat, and they walked towards the exit. She could see some people standing on the other side of the door, waiting for them. She assumed they were all going to eat together at the hotel.

"Sod that," said Spliff, and he suddenly steered her in the opposite direction. For a moment she wondered whether he'd forgotten something, then she realised they were heading for the fire exit.

"You don't mind, do you?" he said, opening

the door and ushering her outside and appearing to assume in his irritating way that she didn't. "I just don't think I could stomach an evening of shop-talk."

She felt totally disorientated. One moment they'd been going out with everyone else, the next moment they'd crossed the forecourt and were through the barrier and out on their own in the street, looking for a taxi.

"Where are we going?" Jessica asked.

"Restaurant. The hotel food is vile."

"I . . . well . . ." She really didn't know what to say.

"Thai? Mexican? Indonesian? What?"

A taxi pulled up beside them. He opened the door for her. She couldn't just stand there, so she got in. He said something to the driver, and got in as well.

"French then," he said to her, "unless you've any objections."

She shook her head, and by shaking her head she'd agreed.

They stopped at a small restaurant. The waiter knew him, and immediately took them to a table in the corner. A couple of people recognised him as they brushed past but he was obviously used to it, just nodded politely and shepherded Jessica to her seat. Their table was completely secluded; they might as well have been on their own.

It was just wine and small-talk to begin with. He knew a lot more about art than she'd expected although he deliberately trivialised what he knew, mispronouncing names and using malapropisms like areola instead of aureolin.

"I don't like completely abstract stuff," he said, "I like to recognise something, legs or tits preferably. Toulouse Latrine, he's all right."

"Anyone contemporary you rate?"

"Bradburne."

"Bradburne?" She'd never heard of him.

"Save of the fucking century against Arsenal. That was a *real* work of art."

"I thought you liked Wittgenstein."

He looked amused. "I'm surprised you've heard of him."

"I've read bits of the *Tractatus*."

He didn't even hesitate. "What's that then, some new fanzine I haven't heard of? They usually send me advance copies."

"You know what it is," said Jessica. "You read it at college, and so did I. Wittgenstein saw language as a tool, though later on he changed his . . . er . . . position and decided it had a vast number of uses."

He smiled, and the yob image just seemed to melt away. "You've been doing some digging of your own, haven't you?" he said. "I've been running this show for more than two years, and nobody's ever really fought back before."

"How do you mean?"

"The only way to get the better of me is to find out as much about me as I've found out about you. And you've only got twenty-four hours. I've had six months."

"Six months?"

He poured some more wine. "Bit of an unequal contest, wouldn't you say?"

"Oh I don't know. Prudence and Louise-Marie have let a few things slip . . ."

"Only their clothes," said Spliff. "They don't know anything else about me. Nothing of any importance."

"That's not what you said earlier."

"What did I say earlier?"

"We're all light bulbs, remember? On, off. As simple as that." Oh the recklessness of alcohol. But she was almost enjoying herself.

He laughed.

"Why do you do it then, if it doesn't mean anything?"

"Do what?"

He was going to make her say it. "Screw around."

"I enjoy it."

"Bit of an unequal contest for them, wouldn't you say?"

"They can always decline."

"Do they?"

He laughed. "No."

Jessica shook her head.

"Listen," said Spliff, "give someone real power and they use it, every time. No exceptions."

She looked at him. "You have enormous

power over me. Tomorrow you're going to change my life for ever, aren't you? How does that make you feel? Knowing what you're going to do?"

"What do you expect me to say?" said Spliff. "Omnipotent? Guilty? *Randy*?"

"You just like baiting people," said Jessica. "You get off on it."

"Dead right," said Spliff, "but don't worry. I may screw my subjects' lives up from time to time but I don't screw *them*."

"Never?"

"Never."

"You surprise me."

"I surprise myself sometimes."

"Why? I mean – you're obviously not frightfully particular, generally speaking."

He smiled.

"Have you ever wanted to?"

"Of course," said Spliff, "but it would be like playing with a hostage. Hostages often fall in love with their kidnappers, people they would normally loathe. Interviewing people is a lot like sex – you look for the erogenous zones. And if they're not immediately apparent, you create them with the appropriate stimulation."

Ten

"Were you really a trucker," asked Jessica, "or was that just hype?"

He smiled. "That's the only bit that *was* true."

He talked about his travels, relating surreal stories about different countries in ludicrous accents and making her laugh. He finished up with one about Amsterdam which she couldn't have repeated to anyone. "Then I was on one of those lorries that was caught in that fiasco in Somalia, and after that I drove a safari bus in Kenya for a while."

Somalia. That had been twelve years ago. "How old are you?" she asked.

"Thirty-seven. Next question."

"Why didn't you ever get married?"

"I did. We split up ages ago. It lasted a bit longer than three days, but not dramatically so."

"Why?"

"I didn't want children. Rosalind did."

"You hadn't discussed it beforehand?"

"She changed her mind. Or her family changed her mind for her. Rosalind's family were a bit like the bloody mafia; there were far too many of them and they all hated one another. You need to follow up each answer quickly with another question Jessica, that's how you interview people. Don't give the subject a chance to reflect."

"Did you love her?"

He shrugged.

"You must have told her you did."

"No," said Spliff. "I follow the rules of good broadcasting; if I have trouble with a phrase I never use it." He poured some more wine and then the food arrived and they started to eat, talking between mouthfuls. The conversation started to take unexpected twists and turns; a mystery tour of interlocking experiences. They hummed some of the animals from *Peter and the Wolf*, circled the pyramids, got emotional about conservation issues and discussed the structure of language.

"Rosalind was a linguist," he said. "She saw me as a long-term translation project."

"Did she get any further than page three?"

He laughed. "She didn't speak the right lingo."

"What is the right lingo?"

"Ah," said Spliff, "that's one you'll have to work out on your own. What languages do you speak?"

"French and Spanish. You know that."

"I suspect you speak another one," he said. "We'll see." He ran his finger rather sensually round the rim of his glass.

She flushed.

He shook his head. "I didn't mean sex."

She was so sure that was what he *had* meant that she was taken aback for a moment, and then intrigued. She realised she was enjoying herself; he was really good company, she was forgetting who he was. The studio seemed a long way away. She watched his face for a moment and was surprised to see someone she rather liked, who only bore a passing resemblance to the man in front of the camera.

"What do you think of television today?" he asked suddenly.

"Not much," said Jessica.

"What do you watch?"

"Very little, actually. I don't think you learn very much as a passive spectator." But I'm not a spectator any longer, am I, she thought. I'm a participant. "I like old films," she added.

He slid his glass along the table, studying it. "Television reflects the preoccupations of a society, feeds them back into the system and exaggerates them in the process. Then we all feel we're getting a little bit less than everyone else, and the advertisers clean up. What else do you watch?"

"I don't watch documentaries because they're all biased."

"How do you know?"

"Oh come on, pollution investigations sponsored by oil companies? Medical programmes paid for by pharmaceutical giants?"

"Did you watch the one on surrogacy?"

"You're joking," said Jessica. "It was funded by a group of fertility clinics."

"What else do you watch?"

"Wildlife programmes, drama . . ."

"What drama?"

"Well, there was that one a couple of months back about a celebrity chef . . ."

"Any good?"

"Not really."

"Did you read any plays at school?"

"*Hedda Gabler* and *A Midsummer Night's Dream*. I saw a couple of other Shakespeare plays with my parents. And then I read a lot." She pushed her plate away. "What sort of school did you go to?"

"Minor public."

"Latin and Greek?"

"Latin and Greek."

"So you don't come from a sink estate, and you didn't go to the local correction centre."

"Nope. My parents were comfortably off, not as rich as yours but OK." He moved his glass of Chardonnay so that she could see his hand through it. "What do you see in there?"

"Your fingers."

"Do they look like my fingers?"

"No. The liquid is distorting and discolouring

them."

"So they're not my fingers."

"Yes they are. You couldn't remove your hand and leave that image behind."

"But it's not a truthful image. It's larger than life, for one thing."

"It has an essence of truth."

"In vino veritas?"

"Depends on the wine," said Jessica.

"Let's take it further," he said. He drank half the contents of the glass and put it back on the table. "What do you see now?"

"Still your fingers. But the tops of them aren't misshapen any more. The rest of them are as peculiar as ever."

He drank the rest of the wine and put the glass back again.

"Nearly back to normal," said Jessica.

"And when I remove the glass entirely?" He slid it to one side. "Very few people see me without it."

She suddenly realised that he was representing television with the glass, and himself with just his hand. The wine was the tunnel-vision bureaucracy that permeated every area of life. "So why are you showing *me* the man behind the TV screen?" she said.

He hesitated. "Because I think you deserve to know who you're really dealing with."

She fiddled with her dessertspoon. Despite the underlying warning he'd made her feel singular and special again.

"Why did your engagement only last three days?" he asked.

"I thought you knew everything about me. One of the cardinal rules of interviewing people. Don't ask a question unless you already know the answer."

"I break the rules," said Spliff. "That's why I'm so good. Now answer the question. Why?"

"You were right about the light bulb," said Jessica, realising she was too drunk to monitor what she was saying and not caring anyway. "He couldn't find the switch."

"Has anyone found it?"

"You don't talk about something as simplistic as the position of a light switch to a qualified electrician," said Jessica.

"I've been called a lot of things," said Spliff, "but that's never been one of them. Vampire, vulture, viper . . . never electrician. You've scored a first there."

"You forgot the lowest common denominator."

She realised that the more laid-back he looked, the closer he was watching.

"You have worked fast, haven't you?" he said lazily. "Prudence ought to take lessons. Got a photograph of the bruises as well?"

The waiter cleared away their plates and brought the coffee.

"Why is this particular programme so

important to you?" asked Jessica.

"Can't we talk about something else? It may be riveting for you, but it's just work for me."

"People's lives," said Jessica dismissively. "Just work."

They both reached for the cream at the same time, and their hands brushed. She felt the hairs on her arms rise with the charge, as though she'd touched a nylon shirt and had a dose of static electricity.

"You've got some odd interests," said Spliff. "Entomology, botany . . ."

It was unnerving when he came out with things he knew about her, things she hadn't told him. "Subject matter for paintings," she said. She finished her coffee.

"What shall we do now?" said Spliff. "The night is relatively young, and the stars are doing their thing . . ."

"Twinkling . . ."

"Twinkling. And I want to forget all about television."

Jessica pushed her cup away, stood up and took a deep breath. Then she said, "Is this my last night as Jessica Pierce?"

"That's work," said Spliff quickly.

"It's my *life*," said Jessica.

"It's mine too, as it happens," said Spliff, standing up as well.

"My life, or your life?"

He cupped his hands together. "Both. Come

on, let's go."

They left the restaurant and walked for a few minutes, although neither of them mentioned a destination. Suddenly Spliff stopped and said, "Let's do something mad."

"What?"

He thought for a moment. Then he said, "Badgers."

"Badgers?"

"I've got a mate with a farm in Surrey." He looked at his watch. "Forty minutes from Waterloo . . . he could meet us at the other end . . . yeah. Why not. I'll ring him." He got out his mobile.

"What's he like, this friend?" asked Jessica, as the train pulled away.

"Someone I've known since I was a kid."

This should be interesting, thought Jessica. "Schoolfriend?"

"Hmm. Don't mention reindeer."

"Why not?"

"His name's Rudolph." He put his hands behind his head and closed his eyes.

A lanky hoodie stopped in the aisle, and rested his hand on the back of the seat. He had teeth tattooed on his knuckles. "You're Spliff, ain't yer?" he said.

Spliff opened his eyes and gave a tired smile.

"Why were you such a bastard to that chick?"

"Which one?"

"You know which one. The one who found out her dog wasn't a pedigree. I've got a dog."

"Everyone should have a hobby."

"She's a Rottweiler bitch."

"I guessed as much."

"Are you taking the piss?"

"Me? No," said Spliff.

"Are you really into *Dracula's Dentures*?"

"You betcha."

"What's your favourite track?"

"*You Drive a Stake Through My Heart*," replied Spliff. "It has very pointed lyrics."

"Yeah. Right."

"Well," said Spliff, after a long pause, "nice to have met you."

The youth stood there for a moment, then he turned round and sauntered back to his mates. "It *was* him," Jessica heard him say. A couple of spotty faces peered over the backs of their seats, and quickly disappeared again when they saw she was looking.

It had been a very odd experience, that little exchange. Spliff had been so in control of the whole thing that she could still feel the thrill of being associated with him; it rubbed off like gold-dust, she was still glittering with it.

"It gets to be a drag in the end," said Spliff.

"Who in God's name are *Dracula's Dentures*?

"Classic-Vampire-Scratch splinter group. I do my homework."

Eleven

The man who met them at the station was tall and thin, and he had a wispy beard. He had very penetrating bright blue eyes and wore a tweed jacket that was falling apart.

"Ye gods," he said, looking at Jessica, "a woman. You didn't say there'd be two of you."

"Didn't I?"

"You old bastard," said Rudolph. "Who is she, then?"

"Meet Rudolph," said Spliff. "He's harmless."

"He hasn't brought a woman down here for . . . Jesus, I don't know how long. Here . . ." He gave her a leg-up into his Land Rover. The step was missing.

They drove off into the night. "So who are you then?" enquired Rudolph. "Spliff didn't say."

"Jessica Pierce," said Spliff, before Jessica

could answer.

"Christ," said Rudolph, missing a gear, "is this wise?"

Spliff didn't answer.

"It's fucking stupid, that's what it is," said Rudolph, neatly avoiding a hedgehog. "No offence, Jessica, but . . . bloody *hell*, Spliff. It's half past eleven now, you've got to be back at the studio by ten in the morning. She doesn't have to be in until the afternoon."

He seemed to know a lot about it.

"We've come down here to look at the badgers," said Spliff. "All discussions about work are strictly off-limits."

"I'm not surprised," said Rudolph, with a dark look in Spliff's direction. "You astound even me sometimes."

Jessica wondered how much he knew. Quite a bit, she decided.

"I've got sacks of chicken-feed all over the living room," Rudolph went on, "and I'm not sodding moving them at this time of night so you'll both have to use the spare room." He switched on *The Mikado* and the three of them sang Gilbert and Sullivan songs all the way to the farm, changing the words from time to time and bursting out laughing.

"I'm not coming out to see the bloody things," said Rudolph, "I'm going to bed. You know where everything is. You're mad, you know that don't you; both of you, mad as hatters. Goodnight Spliff.

Goodnight victim."

Spliff carried the flashlight, Jessica the binoculars, and they made their way across a couple of fields. The moon was nearly full, and there was only the occasional wisp of cloud in the sky. It hadn't rained for some time, and they settled themselves down in a little hollow so that they could just see over the rim in the direction of the set.

"Whoever would have thought it," said Jessica, looking up at the stars. "In the middle of a bloody field." She shivered, although it wasn't particularly cold.

"Here," said Spliff, reaching into his pocket.

He handed her a hipflask of whisky, and she took a couple of sips.

"He's left this field fallow because of the badgers," said Spliff, taking a swig himself. "Mind you, he probably gets a whacking great subsidy for doing so. He's got batboxes in the trees."

"*Hoo hoo hoo*" from the sycamore beside them. "Tawny owl," said Jessica.

"Very good," said Spliff.

"We used to have one in the garden," said Jessica. "What sort of a house did you grow up in?"

"1930s, horrible curved windows with metal frames. Bauhaus for beginners."

"Did you like school?"

"Nope."

"Why not?"

"I was small and fat and I got bullied."

She couldn't imagine anyone bullying him. He was too quick, the sort of person who always manages to turn whatever weapon you use back on yourself. "So you do know what it's like to be a victim," she said.

"You can't reduce all human behaviour to reactions to circumstances." He sounded slightly annoyed. "I am not a determinist – I have to believe I have a say in what I do."

She glanced across at him. He wasn't looking at her any more; his face was quite serious and he looked utterly different from the person in the studio. A much darker version, who actually thought about what he did and *still* went through with it.

"Rudolph was right," he said suddenly, "it was a bloody idiotic thing to do, bringing you down here." He took another shot of whisky. "Do you make friends with the turkey each Christmas?"

She grinned. "No. I just stuff it."

He laughed.

"Are we friends?" said Jessica.

"I've never sung *Tit Willow* with anyone from work, that's for sure."

"And is it going to be bad news for the turkey tomorrow?"

"Yes," he said simply.

Trussed, stuffed, basted and roasted. She decided not to think about it. There was a faint scuffling in the direction of the set.

"Look." He pushed the binoculars across to

her.

She looked. Two badgers were snuffling around outside, their fat little bodies jostling one another as they nosed the scraps that Rudolph left for them each evening. She watched for a few minutes, entranced, then she gave him back the binoculars. He took them and watched them for a while himself. They didn't speak, although the owl made a couple of comments from the tree. The badgers vanished.

"We were quite lucky there," said Spliff. "You don't always get to see them." He rolled onto his back and looked up at the sky. "That's Polaris." He pointed. "How could anyone call a nuclear missile after something as beautiful as a star?"

"Why do you do *Missing Link*, Spliff?"

He turned his head towards her. They were both lying on their backs, about six feet apart. There was an odd sort of intimacy about it.

"I didn't think it would turn out the way it did," he said. "I kept thinking – another couple of months and then I'll quit if it isn't going more my way. I managed a couple of decent episodes, but Tree went to Potty Noodle and complained."

"Potty Noodle? Who's Potty Noodle?"

"Strickland, the big boss."

"Why Potty Noodle?"

"Convoluted and tasteless. I had a warning from him, something about viewer boredom parameters and audience expectations needing to co-habit with advertising requirements. So I got rid of Tree."

"How?"

"Oh, it's easy," said Spliff. "You just delegate where you shouldn't until no one knows who they're answerable to any more. Chaos."

"So what do you intend to do now he's gone?"

"I might get a telescope," said Spliff.

Jessica smiled, and decided not to contest the evasion. "What I like about the sky," she said, "is that it can be any colour at all. I remember this beach . . . as the sun went down both the sea and the sky turned green, a sort of pale lime green – so all the shadows went purple, plum-coloured. I wish I'd had a camera."

"Why didn't you paint it?"

"Because it would only be my interpretation. It was the real thing that got to me."

"If you can't have the real thing isn't a facsimile better than nothing?"

"Not always."

"So there are some things that art cannot serve?"

She wondered precisely what he meant. "I don't know. I haven't really thought about it before."

He passed her the whisky again. "What are you going to do with the rest of your life, Jessica?"

She smiled. "It rather depends on what happens tomorrow, doesn't it?"

"No," he said, "it shouldn't depend on that at all." He sat up. "When I was your age I wanted to be an actor."

"That sounds very condescending," said Jessica. *"When I was your age."*

He looked surprised. "It wasn't meant to be. I got very pretentious, wore black all the time and pondered a lot."

"Hamlet's about indecision," said Jessica. *"You're* the most decisive person I've ever met. You'd have come home from Wittenburg, skewered Claudius immediately, taken the throne, given your mother a good ticking-off and screwed Ophelia. You wouldn't even have waited for the ghost."

He laughed. "Who do you see me as, then?"

"Richard the Third."

"I asked for that, didn't I?"

"Just a bit."

He passed her the flask.

"You're not the person I thought you were at all," said Jessica.

"Nor are you," said Spliff. "We had an art student on once before. She wasn't any good, just another rich talentless twit filling in time. I'd assumed you were going to be the same. I was wrong."

The compliment warmed her even more than the whisky.

"Personally, I'd give anything to be able to play the *Tchaikovsky Violin Concerto*. Those high notes are almost unbearable, the last knife-edge of pleasure before it turns to pain."

Something screeched in the black woods to

their left. Love song or death cry, thought Jessica, I've no idea which. Spliff turned his head towards it and she wondered if he was thinking the same.

"Did you learn the violin, then?" she said.

"I tried the cello for a while. Useless. All rhythm and no pitch. Music and art are two sides of a coin that has always eluded me."

"Art is a quest," said Jessica.

"A quest for what?"

"For what makes the practitioner unique."

"Any conclusions?"

"No," said Jessica, "have you come to any by your route?"

"Not really."

"So what *is* you, then?"

"I don't know," said Spliff.

They looked at one another, slightly appalled at the turn the conversation had taken. A moth skittered out of the shadow of a tree, zigzagged crazily around in the moonlight and disappeared once again into the gloom. She could see that the image was not lost on him, either.

"I don't think it matters," said Jessica.

"It matters," said Spliff.

"Why?" said Jessica. "I don't believe I have a soul. But I still think I'm unique."

"But programmed."

"If you like."

He shook his head. "You can live without an arm. You can live without a leg. But supposing someone cut you in half, right down the middle." He picked a stalk of rye-grass and tried to split it into two with his thumbnail. It wouldn't oblige. He threw it down, annoyed. "Is it possible for the thing you call *you* to go into both bits, be two different entities at once?"

Jessica thought about it. "No. But then, I'm not sure that all this entity business isn't just an illusion."

"What is reality anyway?" He looked mildly disappointed.

"Don't be so patronising," said Jessica. "I look on myself as a biological system, lots of cells acting in symbiosis." It was getting tricky to make her mouth say what her head intended.

The owl hooted again.

"It must be nice," said Spliff, "to be an owl. All you have to worry about is voles."

"And eggs."

He sat up rather abruptly. "We ought to make a move."

Jessica stood up. The field wheeled around her for a moment, then steadied.

"You OK?"

She nodded.

They started to walk back to the farm, finishing off the whisky as they went. Every time she took another swallow she remembered too late that she'd had enough, and once or twice she stumbled. It would have been so easy to take hold of his arm, natural even. She put her hands in her pockets. The path seemed to zigzag, although it had been straight on the way out.

"You're not really used to this, are you?" said Spliff.

He had to help her over the stile, and once again the touch of his hand did something electric to her. They let themselves into the kitchen, tripped over a cat or two and tried to tiptoe up the stairs.

"Hang on," whispered Spliff, "I think you'd better drink some water. You'll feel like shit in the morning if you don't."

Twelve

Fern put her hot chocolate on the bedside table, and set her alarm clock. Then she laid out the new underwear she'd bought for the next day. She'd been a bit extravagant, red satin and black lace, but she'd recently seen a film where a woman had got stuck in a lift with a film star. With the lack of ventilation it had become so hot in there that they'd had to take their clothes off. Fern did a few exercises to strengthen her tummy muscles, smeared viscous pale blue cream all over her face and climbed into bed.

She sat there for a while, sipping her nightcap and thinking about the next day. *Missing Link* was the most exciting thing that had ever happened to her, she was going to be on *television*. Her mind began to wander, and before long she was stuck in a lift with Spliff and the thermometer was rising fast. She turned off the light and lay down.

She could hear the rumble of lorries on the

main road; it went on nearly all night, every night. She remembered one woman on *Missing Link* who'd been given a ticket to visit new-found relatives in South Africa. A holiday. Wouldn't that just be brilliant?

It was another two hours before she fell asleep and by that time the lift had jammed eight times and she'd met five film stars, two millionaires and a racing car driver.

* * *

"There's only one bed," said Spliff. "I'll sleep on the couch by the window. There's a spare quilt."

"You don't have to," said Jessica.

"I do have to," said Spliff.

"I didn't mean . . ."

"I know you didn't." He sat on the end of the bed and took his shoes off.

All of a sudden Jessica wanted to cry. It's the whisky, she thought, I don't really want to go to bed with him. Like hell you don't, said a little voice inside her head.

"I'm fifteen years older than you," said Spliff, "I know what I'm doing. Not doing." He stripped down to a T-shirt and underwear, and she did the same. They said goodnight.

She was very aware of his body on the other side of the room. The dark patch of his hair on the cushion, his arm, slightly bent, very white in the moonlight. The faint sound of his breathing. She had no idea who went to sleep first.

Rudolph barged in with two cups of coffee at eight o'clock the next morning. Spliff pulled the quilt over his head and said, "Fuck off, Rudolph."

Rudolph looked back and forth at Spliff on the sofa, and Jessica in the bed. Then he just said, "Astonishing," and walked out.

"I suppose you want a lift to the station," said Rudolph a bit later, over toast and marmalade.

"Jessica doesn't have to come," said Spliff. "You could show her the adders. We don't need her in the studio until two."

"Delighted," said Rudolph. "All right with you?"

"Fine," said Jessica, trying not to feel disappointed. She'd been looking forward to Spliff's company on the train journey back; there were so many things she wanted to talk to him about all of a sudden.

"Right then," said Spliff, putting on his jacket. They all walked out to the Land Rover.

He turned to Jessica at the last moment, caught her by the wrist and pulled her to him. "This is purely selfish," he said, "because I won't get another chance." Then he kissed her. It didn't last very long, but it was shamelessly erotic. She noticed that Rudolph's face was like thunder as he started the vehicle.

She felt decidedly odd, as though she'd just

found out that the perfectly ordinary car she'd been driving for the last few years was, in fact, capable of going from nought to sixty in under five seconds. Then they were gone, and she was left standing there in the farmyard wishing they hadn't.

She went back into the farmhouse and started to browse through the bookcase. She noticed a volume called *The Joy of Frogspawn*, by someone called Rudolph Myers. She opened the jacket and there was a photograph of Rudolph, younger, holding a frog and looking knowledgeable. She put it back and carried on looking.

She hadn't been quite sure what she was looking for, but as soon as she saw it she knew. A photograph album.

The first few were baby pictures, presumably of Rudolph. She flicked through until she came to one of two teenage boys. She recognised Spliff straight away, but it was the background that caught her attention – a 1930s detached house, with curved windows and metal window frames. A woman was gardening, close to the house. Jessica looked closer. She was stooping over some white chrysanthemums and there was something stiff about her, arthritic; she had thick ankles that bulged over her shoes like soufflés. Spliff's grandmother?

And then a lot of things began to make sense. It wasn't Spliff's grandmother at all. It was his mother, and she must have been a similar age to Jessica's mother, though nothing like as well-preserved. A car door slammed. Jessica put the album back, and went to meet Rudolph.

"Right," said Rudolph, "what do you want to know? He speaks French, German, Russian, Swahili, and metaphor. He's particularly fluent at metaphor."

She stared at him.

"He's given you the opportunity to research him," said Rudolph. "Don't waste it. He hasn't done anything like this before."

"You know what's going to happen, don't you?" said Jessica.

"Only vaguely." She knew he was lying. "But I can fill you in on his background, and then maybe . . . just maybe . . . you'll understand." He filled the kettle. "We first met when we were seven, not long after his father died. I didn't get to meet his mother for ages – always some excuse. He had no idea of how to deal with other children, no idea at all. 'Victim – please kick' written all over him. He changed beyond belief over the next few years. Became the class clown, did wicked impersonations and wrote scurrilous verse about the teachers. He got me into trouble as well because I couldn't help laughing. But by the time he was seventeen he'd made one very important discovery – he could read people like no one else I've ever met. Spliff could tell you what people were going to say before they said it; it was uncanny."

"What was she like, his mother?"

"Terrifying. You had to decode her face to know what she really meant when she said something;

that's where he got the practice."

Rudolph made a pot of tea and washed up a couple of mugs. "We both got offers from Oxford. Spliff was buggering about as usual, doing no revision. He never revised, and he always came top. His mother put her foot down one day and said he wasn't to go out. He said 'fuck you', or something like that, and went."

Rudolph poured the tea.

"When he came back he found her on the kitchen floor, dead. Heart attack." He put the mugs on the table and sat down. "He went a bit loopy after that, screwed his exams and went to a redbrick. We lost contact. When we met up again he'd got involved in the dramatic society and he wanted to be an actor. He got a first, taught for a while and did bit parts. Then he packed up everything and went abroad, trucking, teaching, digging roads. I got the occasional postcard. When he came back he'd changed again. He'd discovered his ability to read people had a physical side, and when he went to bed with someone he could get all the appreciation he'd never had as a child. He's been like a bloody rabbit ever since."

"Did he ever talk about his mother's death?"

"Not to me. Not to anyone, I'd imagine."

"He said he was married once, and it broke up because he didn't want children."

"And because he screwed around," said Rudolph. "No, maybe I'm being a bit unfair. She screwed around as well."

"What was she like?"

Rudolph sighed. "He is a bastard sometimes. He shouldn't have kissed you."

Jessica blushed.

"Drink your tea," said Rudolph. "It's getting cold."

She drank.

"After he came back from Africa," Rudolph went on, "he started getting little acting jobs again, and then he landed Jimmy Crushit in *Balls*. But it was the hooligan element that stuck, and not the fact that he'd been playing a part. They offered him *The Red Card Game* and he took it, thinking it would just be a stop-gap. He was so bloody good at it that the programme just ran and ran, and he ended up representing nearly everything he hated. By then he was hooked on television. When they offered him *Missing Link* he jumped at it, thinking he could mould it his way. But it turned into the biggest thing to hit the ratings for years, and he was stuck with it the way it was – and he was stuck with Simon Tree."

"What did he really want to do?"

"Question the system."

"And now Tree's gone Spliff can do anything he wants."

"Maybe."

"Maybe?" said Jessica. "Don't you know? I thought you knew everything."

Rudolph shook his head. "Not everything. And I don't ask, because I know he feels shitty about some of the things he's done. But you never know with

Spliff; if *Missing Link* isn't going the way he wants he can change the rules mid-sentence and send the whole thing off in a different direction. I've watched him do it. If you want to wrong-foot him you could try accusing him of having a personal angle. He's not *allowed* to have a personal angle."

"It's all getting a bit confrontational," said Jessica. "Do you know anything about the other subject?"

"I haven't met her, if that's what you mean."

"Her," said Jessica, smiling.

"Shit," said Rudolph. He looked at her for a moment. "Actually," he said, "you and Spliff are quite a good match for one another in a funny sort of way. Now let's go and look for snakes. There's this pile of brushwood they like. Adder Mansions, I call it."

He dropped her at the station a couple of hours later. She sat on the train and thought. Spliff was up to something, that much was clear. Something Clive didn't know about was going to happen that evening, live, on air.

She tried to organise the information she had. Spliff had been interested in her painting, but it wasn't dominating things, his antipathy towards elderly parents and only children had been much more to the purpose. Jessica's father might have had a dishonest past, and her mother might not be who she said she was at all . . . But there was a video of Jessica's birth, her mother *had* to be her mother. And Spliff had done his best to make sure the likeness between Jessica and her father was apparent, so her father had to be her father. Aaron Klein figured somewhere, so did the American girl in Costa Rica, so did Spliff's contempt for contemporary television, and so did the woman with the appalling haircut she'd seen earlier, walking down the corridor.

And whatever the link with that woman was, it was something nasty.

Thirteen

"What happened to you last night?" asked Louise-Marie, as Spliff walked into the studio. "Prudence was well pissed off."

"Where's my running order?" said Spliff abruptly.

Louise-Marie glanced at Sandra.

Sandra produced a clipboard.

"What are you doing in here?" demanded Spliff. "You're meant to be minding Fern."

"She's throwing up," said Sandra. "She's really looking forward to meeting you."

Louise-Marie laughed.

"I'll go and see if she's OK, shall I?" said Sandra.

"Do you seriously need me to tell you that?"

Sandra went.

"What's biting you?" said Louise-Marie to Spliff.

"Nothing."

"Don't give me that shit."

"You can be replaced," said Spliff.

She had no idea whether or not he was joking. She walked away.

Louise-Marie had fallen for Spliff in quite a big way the year before. She was good at studio politics, and she had realised that sleeping with him was essential.

She had expected a fairly pedestrian experience – she was new to the studio, and she hadn't really talked to him for more than a couple of minutes. She knew about his reputation, although she couldn't quite square it with his appearance; why on earth did everyone seem to fancy him?

A crowd of them went back to his flat after a show one night. They all got rather stoned, and played a silly quiz game with forfeits. His general knowledge surprised her. She stayed in the kitchen when everyone else left and did some washing up – a considerable sacrifice, because she broke two nails in the process.

When she was quite sure the last person had gone she went back into the lounge and said, "Oh. Where is everyone?"

Spliff was sitting on the settee, reading some magazine called *Nature*. Where to find the best nudist beaches, no doubt. He looked up and smiled, and she realised he'd known she was in the kitchen all the time. She didn't quite know what to say – *Merde, is that the time?* seemed a bit inappropriate, as it was rapidly becoming apparent that he wasn't quite the prat she'd thought he was.

The moment he kissed her she threw her previous expectations out of the window; he became a completely different person. He knew that sex was about perception and imagination, and he had plenty of both. Nobody had ever made her feel quite so much herself, and having found herself, she lost herself completely.

He never slept with her again. This annoyed her more than anything, so she made a play for Stuart Miller and got him. She didn't quite know how she felt about Spliff these days. There wasn't really a word for it.

Well, thought Sandra, as she walked across the studio floor with Fern, at least the red dress is an improvement on the lilac one. She still looks like a sheepdog, though, peering through that ridiculous curtain of pale hair.

Fern could see Spliff sitting on the white leather chair, reading his notes. He glanced up, noticed Sandra, then Fern, and stood up. Fern was surprised, she'd expected him to be taller. Close up he looked older as well.

"Hello," said Spliff. "You must be Fern."

"Hello," said Fern. Her eyes strayed to the scenery; she'd seen it so often on a TV screen, but this was the real thing. It all looked so glamorous, the heavy silver chain design, the lights, the cameras, the sparkling glass table with the froth of white flowers in the centre.

"Shall we get started?"

She smiled weakly and sat down.

"Welcome back after the break," said Spliff. "Now it's time to introduce you to our second guest, Fern Marshall, a reflexologist from London. Fern, you were born in 1983. Liverpool were top of the first division – no premier league then – and you could still buy beer in pints. Tell us a bit about your earliest memories."

"Well . . ." She couldn't think of anything at all. The silence ticked in her head.

"There was an incident at infant school, wasn't there, in the nativity play . . ."

She gulped. Nothing was going to come out.

"Don't worry," said Spliff, "you'll be fine. Once you get started."

Out of the corner of her eye she saw Sandra give him a filthy look.

"Let's try it again," said Spliff. "There was an incident at infant school, wasn't there, when you were five, you were playing Joseph in the . . ."

"Mary."

"Mary." He smiled. "You dropped the baby in the hay . . ."

"I dropped the frankincense in the hay." She was smiling as well now.

"What happened then?"

"Well . . . Joseph called me a silly bitch, and the audience started laughing. So I said, I don't see why we have to have a Joseph anyway. He isn't even Jesus's daddy. He's Mary's boyfriend."

Spliff grinned. "There was just you and your mother at home, wasn't there Fern? A single parent family. Although from time to time there were . . . visitors."

Oh yes. One in the eye for you, Mother. "My mother had lots of boyfriends," said Fern.

"Did you get on with them?"

"Some of them. Dermot was nice."

"Frankie. Do you remember Frankie?"

"He was OK as well," said Fern, surprised that Spliff was only bringing up the good ones. She wanted her mother to wriggle a bit. "He mended my bike for me. The one her previous bloke smashed up when he was legless."

"You don't like your mother a lot, do you?" said Spliff.

She stared at him, open-mouthed. She hadn't expected it to be put as baldly as that.

"Let me rephrase that," said Spliff. "You and your mother fall out from time to time, don't you?"

"Yes."

"And have you fallen out with her at the moment?"

"Yes."

"Why?"

"I can't remember." She couldn't, either.

Spliff put down his clipboard. "I need a cup of coffee," he said. "Where's Prudence?"

A couple of people shrugged.

"I'll get you one," said Sandra quickly.

"I need to stop for a moment," said Spliff. "I'll get it."

Fern watched him go. "Was it something I said?" she asked.

"Of course not," said Sandra, "just something technical. You're doing fine. He's really pleased with you."

Louise-Marie pushed open the swing door of the make-up room. Spliff was sitting in one of the chairs, his hands behind his head; he turned to see who had come in.

"What are you doing in here?" asked Louise-Marie.

"I didn't expect her to be such a *dork*," he said. "Yeah, yeah, I read all the info, I just didn't see how I could get it so wrong . . . Not *twice*, in one show. Jesus Christ, I'm slipping."

"Fern's a lot better than some you've had."

"She wants to punish her mother in front of twenty million people."

"You punish people in front of twenty million people every week."

He smiled sarcastically. "Only consenting adults."

"Come off it. Your contestants have no idea what they're giving their consent to. They just sign a disclaimer."

"Don't we all. I hereby agree to give up all rights to my personal beliefs."

Louise-Marie had never seen him quite like this before. "This is about Jessica, isn't it?" she said slowly. "An attack of conscience. *Quelle surprise*. Hang out the flags. But why this one? Why Jessica, when there've been so many others? She's nothing special."

"Oh, for Christ's sake," said Spliff, "Jessica and I have got a lot in common."

"I'd have expected something rather less clichéd from *you*," said Louise-Marie tartly.

"You don't understand." He was getting angry.

"No, I don't. You've never had any problems before, but you're playing this one very close to your hairy little chest. I *know* you."

"No you don't," said Spliff. "We just fucked, you and me, we didn't *talk*."

She glared at him. "You didn't want anything else. You never do."

He picked up a phial of eyeliner and twirled it between his fingers. "Tear-proof," he said, "of course." He hurled it to the other end of the room. The little glass bottle broke, and a dull purple splashed against the wall and trickled down it like venous blood.

Louise-Marie stared. "She's really got to you,

hasn't she? Good God. Where were you last night?"

"I didn't sleep with her. This is about something else."

"What?"

"Why did Fern have to be such a dork?" repeated Spliff.

"She isn't a dork," said Louise-Marie. "I don't know what's got into you. Why does it matter so much? They need never see one another again after today."

He kicked the rubbish bin viciously and walked out.

"OK?" said Spliff.

Fern nodded.

"After Frankie there was . . ." he looked at his notes, "Max. He used to make you cry, didn't he?"

Fern began to feel uncomfortable.

"What made you cry, Fern?"

His persistence was making her cross, and when she got cross she got reckless. "What makes *you* cry?" she retorted.

"Tchaikovsky's Violin Concerto."

"Hold it," said Clive.

Spliff turned to him with exaggerated politeness. "Don't worry," he said, "it'll be canaries instead of violins tonight."

Clive nodded. Spliff's antipathy towards both the yellow strip of Norwich City and Norwich City itself was a running gag.

Spliff turned back to Fern. "How did this string of boyfriends make you feel about men in general?"

"You couldn't trust them," she said, wondering if he'd got the canary wrong. They'd had a parrot.

"But you did trust Karl, didn't you?"

How the hell did he know about Karl? She hadn't written it down on the form they'd sent her.

"Tell us about Karl."

"I'd rather not," said Fern.

"Hold it a minute," said Spliff. He went over to the sofa, sat down next to Fern and put his arm round her. "I know this isn't going to be easy for you," he said, "but I like to think this show is about helping people come to terms with difficult things in their past. By talking about this, you'll be helping other women. I know it's hard, but just think of all those victims out there who've kept secrets for years, who'll think – if *she* can be that brave, then so can I."

There was something so reassuring about his body; warm, cuddly, paternal – but not *too* paternal. "I'll do whatever you want," she said.

"I know you will," said Spliff. He gave her a brief squeeze and went back to his seat.

Fourteen

"Have you heard?" said Sandra to Louise-Marie. "Potty Noodle is coming tonight."

Sandra was the beauty of the studio, no question; she usually wore a tracksuit and trainers, and she made them look like *haute couture*.

"What a night to choose," said Louise-Marie.

"Why? Do you know something I don't?"

"Just a feeling," said the French girl. "Spliff isn't himself. He says he didn't screw that Jessica girl, but she didn't stay in her hotel last night. Prudence is meant to be keeping an eye on her and she can't find her."

"Curiouser and curiouser," said Sandra.

"Spliff was in the make-up room, just sitting there. If I didn't know him better I'd think he was . . . oh, I don't know. Did you hear that sickly little spiel he gave Fern, about baring your soul for the benefit of the audience?"

Sandra smiled. "Yes."

Louise-Marie glanced down at her perfect nails. "Sandra, how many times did you . . . er . . ."

"Four," said Sandra.

"Oh," said Louise-Marie.

Sandra looked at her.

"Just the once, me."

"I think it was four," said Sandra. As she heard herself say it she thought, who are you trying to kid? Of course it was four, each one different, each one memorable. Four colours.

"I bet," Spliff had said one evening, "I could choreograph a night out where everything was linked to one colour. Give me a colour."

"Blue," said Harry.

"OK," said Spliff. "Now I need a moderator."

"Sandra," said Harry.

"She'll do," said Spliff.

"All right," said Sandra. She only found out later that he'd set it up with Harry; he had no intention of trying out his idea on anyone other than her.

She went along with it all, wearing a tight blue velvet dress and ordering a blue curaçao. She didn't particularly like curaçao, but it looked good. She'd expected him to choose a blue movie, but he didn't. He took her to the NFT and they saw *The Blue Angel*. After that they went to a restaurant called the Sapphire House and had something with a blue cheese sauce.

Sandra was used to the attention she got from men; she expected it, really, and it was always a surprise when someone was interested in her mind as well as her body. They went back to his flat. He'd got hold of a huge bunch of cornflowers, which he'd distributed round the place in jam-jars; they listened to Billie Holiday.

"Ten out of ten," she said to him.

"The question is," said Spliff, running his finger up her thigh and moving the dress up with it, "how blue can we actually get?"

"Ultraviolet, if you like," said Sandra, who was finding him more interesting by the minute.

She knew it wasn't going to be a long-term attachment; he didn't go in for them and she was on the rebound from someone else. Men usually asked her out to be a decoration, a status symbol, as heads would turn wherever she went. Then they couldn't wait to get her into bed and boast about it.

Spliff didn't give a bugger about any of that, and he took his time. It was as though he knew precisely what usually happened, and he was going to show her something else. He started to unravel her, strand by strand, and it took all night. She felt as though someone had taken her to pieces and put her back together again in a slightly different order; she felt good about herself, better than she had for a long time. In the morning she felt affectionate towards him rather than possessive, the way she might have felt towards a therapist, and she was surprised and touched when he suggested doing a different colour a few days later.

"You choose," he said.

"Red."

He looked at her. "Are you sure?"

She nodded, wishing she had the creativity to organise it herself, but all she could think of were red herrings and radishes.

This time they saw a play called *Another Red Shift*; they went back to his flat and he grilled red mullet and they drank red wine. He was an excellent cook.

"What's the riskiest thing you've ever done?" he asked her.

"Parachute jump," said Sandra. Although she was slight she was quite athletic and she had courage. "What about you?"

"Picking strawberries," said Spliff.

"What?" she laughed.

"Red," said Spliff, "so perfectly acceptable. My mother used to make me do it. They were always covered in slugs, and however hard you tried to avoid them you couldn't. They got inside your shoes, up your sleeves, everywhere. You can still scare me witless with a strawberry."

She laughed. "And that's the riskiest thing you've ever done? I doubt it."

"Ah," said Spliff, "it's all a question of perspective."

Some perspective, thought Sandra. She knew

he'd been shot at in Somalia and stranded in the Sahara. She began to wonder about his childhood, and whether he was trying to tell her something. But when she tried to get him to talk about it, he suddenly seemed to change his mind and quickly diverted her attention from the subject by getting physical.

They did green; a day out in the country, with crème de menthe chocolates and Chartreuse. They lay in the grass and ate greengages; then they strolled through the grounds of a deserted farm and Spliff said, "Greenhouse," pointing at a structure that had seen better days.

"We can't," said Sandra, but she knew they were going to.

The path outside was a public footway. Nobody passed, but they could have. She couldn't believe what she'd done, afterwards.

The last colour they did was black; he didn't have to say it was the last, but she knew. She wasn't even particularly sad about it. The whole affair seemed to exist inside a little glass box; something to be taken out and looked at once in a while, but not too often.

"This time," she said, "I want to find out what turns you on."

"There's no mystery about it," said Spliff. "It's arousing you."

"So you're never selfish in bed?"

"Only if you want me to be," said Spliff.

She tried everything she knew that night to make him lose control, but she couldn't manage it.

* * *

Spliff scribbled a couple of things on his notes and looked up at Fern. Fern smiled wanly. "I think it's time we talked about Karl," said Spliff.

"He seemed OK to begin with," said Fern. Then she told him how Karl had raped her, and she didn't leave anything out.

"Thank you," said Spliff. "You were absolutely brilliant."

"My *God*," said Louise-Marie to Sandra. "Did you know that was going to come up?"

Sandra nodded.

"If he's getting this close to the unacceptable this early on in the programme," said Louise-Marie, "what the hell has he got planned for the rest of it?"

Fern was feeling better. Spliff looked pleased with her, and they were getting round to the thing that really interested her.

"You said that Max upset you by pretending to be your father," said Spliff.

She nodded.

"So who was your real father, Fern?"

"I don't know," said Fern.

"You've no idea? You must have looked at your birth certificate."

"There's a blank for father," said Fern.

"Do you think your mother knew who he was?"

"Yes," said Fern, slightly shocked.

"But she wouldn't talk about it?"

"No." She felt sick with excitement. This was going to be *it*, the link, the person she'd never met, it was going to be her father.

"Your marriage broke up, didn't it Fern? Why was that?"

"I couldn't have children. I picked up an infection after I had the abortion. The abortion I had after the rape. I didn't dare go to the doctor's in case he told my mother what I'd done."

Spliff turned a page, and the crackle of paper sounded as though somebody had turned up the amplification somehow. Then Clive said, "I think we could all do with a break."

Spliff stood up. Clive beckoned to him. Spliff walked over. "What's happened to the laughs?" said Clive.

"There never were any," said Spliff.

Prudence appeared.

"You've found out where Jessica is, have you?" said Spliff. "Jolly good."

Prudence looked taken aback. "She rang me from the station. She's gone back to the hotel to have a shower and a change, and she'll be here by two."

"Where had she been?" asked Louise-Marie.

"She didn't say."

Louise-Marie looked at Spliff, but he was completely expressionless.

"Jessica *was* with you, wasn't she?" said Louise-Marie. "*Imbecile.*"

"Last leg," said Clive. "We can all break for lunch after this."

"I don't get to find out what the link is until this evening, do I?" said Fern.

"No," said Spliff.

"I think I might have guessed."

"Clever old you," said Spliff.

Fern beamed.

"OK," said Spliff, "let's get going. We need to know a bit more about your mother, Fern. How old was she when you were born?"

"Twenty-three."

"Did she go to college?"

"Yes, she did Business Studies."

"And after that?"

"She just said she had a series of jobs, nothing terribly exciting."

"So you didn't know she worked for DDI?"

"DDI?" said Fern.

"Just to remind you folks at home," said Spliff, "DDI is the pharmaceutical company that made *Parfromol* . . ." He turned to Fern. "What we're going to do at this point is to ask your mother to come up and sit next to you."

"What?" shrieked Fern. "She's coming this evening? She's going to *be* here?"

Spliff put his hand over hers and squeezed it gently. "She doesn't know you're one of the subjects of tonight's show. Can you handle that?"

"Oh yes," said Fern, as though she'd just been given a blank cheque, "I can handle that." Then something occurred to her. "Spliff," she said, "I hope I haven't fouled up. I sent her a postcard telling her to watch it because I was on it."

He smiled. "I know. But Sandra didn't post it. Now then – I'll introduce your mother, and you move over to let her sit down. Let's try it."

Fern nodded.

"And so," said Spliff, "it's time to meet one of the main protagonists in tonight's story. Fern Marshall's mother, Eveline."

Fifteen

"This is the last *Missing Link* I'm going to do," said Spliff to Harry the cameraman, in the canteen. "And I want to go out with a bang."

Harry stared at him. "You're serious, aren't you? In front of the frigging boss, too. Did you know he was going to be here tonight?"

"I asked him," said Spliff.

Harry took a deep breath. "I see. And we're going out live."

"We always do."

"For the last six months, anyway. It was a good publicity move. Whose idea was it? Yours, I suppose. How long have you been planning this?"

"Two years."

"Oh my God." Spliff could plan mayhem in two minutes. Two years didn't bear thinking about. "What are you going to do – afterwards, I mean?"

"I don't know. I could spend a year or two

travelling. Or I could write a book. Or I could go into politics." He laughed. "No ties. No nothing."

Harry tried a wild card. "Whatever happened to Rosalind?"

"She married a barrister."

"Shame about that."

"No it wasn't," said Spliff. "We loathed one another."

"I liked her," said Harry, instantly wishing he hadn't spoken.

"Oh, I know you did," said Spliff. "It doesn't bug me. It was a long time ago."

"She was only trying to get her own back."

"You still feel you owe me one?"

"You know I do," replied Harry, his heart sinking.

"I want you on *my* camera," said Spliff. "And I want you to stay on me at the end, whatever happens."

"Clive can override me."

"No. It's fixed. I did a little deal with that whizz kid from I.T."

Prudence walked in.

"Aren't you meant to be working?" said Spliff shortly.

"How do you mean?"

"Making sure people don't bump into one another. Is Elspeth here yet?"

"Yes," said Prudence, "she's in her dressing room. I said you'd do the run-through with her at two-thirty. Was that OK?"

"You know it's OK," said Spliff. "I wrote it down for you."

"Oh, yes," said Prudence.

"Is Jessica here yet?" asked Harry.

"No, but it isn't quite two."

Spliff went livid. "You were meant to stick with her!" he shouted. "You should have collected her from the hotel! Supposing she arrives at reception at the same time as someone else?"

Prudence looked scared. People were watching. "I don't think that's likely, is it? And she wouldn't recognise anyone."

"You aren't here to *think*, Prudence, you're here to do as you're told."

Prudence had gone white.

"Get out there and find her," said Spliff.

Prudence looked sick. She left quickly.

"You are edgy, aren't you," said Harry. "Poor old Prudence. Maybe that's one you shouldn't have slept with."

"She'd have felt even worse if she'd been left out."

"Jessica's a nice girl," said Harry.

Spliff didn't say anything. He fiddled with a teaspoon.

"I said, Jessica's a nice girl."

"I heard you the first time," said Spliff.

Harry looked at him. "Oh you haven't . . . I didn't think you ever . . ."

"No," said Spliff, "I haven't. She's nearly young enough to be my daughter."

"Knowing you," said Harry, "are you sure she isn't?"

"Are any of us sure about anything?" said Spliff flippantly. But he got up and put on his jacket and Harry knew he'd said the wrong thing.

Sandra sat on the steps at the bottom of the audience seating, eating a gherkin and anchovy sandwich. She'd got Fern safely stowed away downstairs in her dressing room, and they were just waiting for Patsy to get Elspeth. Suddenly Prudence walked in, followed by Jessica.

"You said I was to find her," said Prudence. "You didn't say what I was to do with her. I thought you meant me to bring her here." She was holding onto Jessica's sleeve as though she was frightened she might run away. Jessica shook her off.

Spliff looked up and their eyes met.

"Hello," said Spliff finally.

"Hello," said Jessica. "I'm not meant to be here, am I?"

"No," said Spliff.

"I'll go then."

"No." Spliff jumped up off the sofa, and rushed over to her, "I want a word first."

"Two minutes," said Clive.

Spliff nodded, and shepherded Jessica to the

make-up room. He shut the door behind them and leant against it.

"Which particular word was it you wanted?" said Jessica.

"Yes or no. Do you want to pull out? Forget anything I said. I'll tear up the disclaimer. Do you want to pull out?"

"Do you want me to?"

"No. Yes. No. I don't know."

"No then. You see, I've worked out what you're going to do."

Spliff's face went very still.

"Not the details," said Jessica, "but you gave me too many clues. You're going to take a stand against something. The programme, the role of television itself maybe. I don't know."

There was a long moment of silence. Then he shook his head. "You ought to tell me to fuck off."

"I'm agreeing to it."

"You don't know what you're agreeing to."

"I agree with your views on the way the media's dumbing down," said Jessica. "I want the chance to be part of something that screams and shouts about it."

He took a deep breath and shut his eyes for a moment, and she didn't know whether he was pleased with what she'd said or sorry. Then he turned round abruptly, opened the door for her and they walked out into the studio. Prudence grabbed Jessica by the elbow and they left for the dressing room.

* * *

"You must be Elspeth," said Spliff. "Come and sit down."

Elspeth sat down, tentatively, as though the sofa might suddenly swallow her up and, worst of all, belch loudly. She was actually there, in a television studio, and it was actually him. His face was a bit more lined than she'd expected, but as soon as he gave her his full attention she felt that no one else existed for him at that moment, that everything she said would be fascinating.

"Elspeth. You've been friends with Jessica for a long time. What sort of a person would you say she is?"

"Gosh," said Elspeth, "she's . . . er . . ."

"Artistic?"

"Yes," said Elspeth, "artistic."

"Did you spend a lot of time round at Jessica's house?"

"No. Yes. Sort of yes and no." There was a trace of panic in her eyes.

Spliff put down his clipboard. "Crocodile," he said.

"What?" said Elspeth.

"It's just a nice word, don't you think? You give me one you think sounds nice."

"Alligator."

"Christmas."

"Goose."

"Make up a sentence with all those four words in it . . . crocodile, alligator, Christmas and goose."

"Er . . . the alligator gave the crocodile a goose for Christmas."

Spliff raised an eyebrow and smiled.

Elspeth put her hand over her mouth. Then she giggled.

"Tell me about the time . . ."

Elspeth started to talk, and Spliff seemed really interested in everything she had to say. She thought he was wonderful.

* * *

Patsy had known Spliff since the days of *The Red Card Game*, before the Botox and the hair extensions – but not before the imaginative underwear. She'd been his gofer, and they'd ended up back at his flat one evening after a show. She'd heard that he wasn't the most difficult of people to pull, and she felt annoyed when he didn't make a move. Eventually she cornered him in the kitchen and goaded him into it.

Patsy had expected him to be rough, wanted him to be, and he was. But there'd been a subtlety behind it she hadn't anticipated; she'd thought she'd be able to drive him to distraction but it was the other way round.

He made it quite clear that it was a one-off, and she resented it. She told him she wasn't on the pill after all, she'd lied about it, so they'd better keep their fingers crossed. For a moment he looked at her as though he could have killed her, then he just went icy. The atmosphere between them at work became impossible, and she left. She worked for a soap for a while, became involved with somebody else, got pregnant, had the baby and found herself on her own with a child to support. She heard about *Missing Link* on the grapevine, and signed the contract before she realised that Spliff was going to be the presenter.

In the event, it hadn't been too awful. He didn't make things difficult for her, and she was careful not to aggravate him in any way.

Sixteen

Prudence and Patsy crossed paths in the corridor as Patsy was taking Elspeth back to her dressing room and Prudence was taking Maureen up to the studio.

"Miss Garvey!" cried Elspeth. "How nice to see you. Isn't all this fun?"

"Whoops," said Patsy.

"I didn't realise you two knew each other," said Prudence. "None of you are meant to know who else is on."

"Spliff's lovely," said Elspeth.

"You surprise me," said Maureen. "Didn't he once describe a goalkeeper as the greatest love of his life?"

"Oh," said Prudence, "that's just . . ." She stopped as Patsy kicked her on the ankle, and then added, ". . . just what any football fan might say." They parted company.

* * *

"Hello," said Spliff, standing up as she crossed the studio floor. "You must be Maureen Garvey. I'm Spliff."

They shook hands. She was slightly taken aback, she hadn't expected that sort of courtesy.

"Just give me a moment," said Spliff, scribbling something down, "and we'll be away."

She studied him as he wrote. He wrote very quickly, small neat letters, and he used an old-fashioned fountain pen. He could do with losing a bit of weight but it wasn't off-putting, it made him look cuddly. She'd expected tattoos or earrings or gold chains but there weren't any; all he wore was a watch, and a very expensive one at that. He put his pen down on the table, looked up at her and smiled.

She was surprised again. His eyes were quite unusual, light grey, and there was a sophistication behind them she hadn't expected at all. Nice mouth. She knew the smile was calculated to appeal to an elderly lady; faintly deferential, very reassuring and yet . . . there was something almost flirtatious about it. He didn't quite fall into the category she'd allotted him.

"You're a football fan I believe," she said.

"That's right," said Spliff.

"And into all that horrid music?"

He laughed. "Yes."

"And your name is another word for a joint."

There was a slight change of expression in his eyes. "Yours is another name for bitterness, isn't it?"

She smiled. "Touché, young man." He was absolutely right. Maureen, as a derivation of Mary, was Hebrew for bitterness.

"Can we get on?" called Clive.

"Yeah, yeah," said Spliff. "And now it's time to introduce you all to Maureen Garvey, Jessica's aunt, the only relative she seems to have left. Those beautiful blue eyes are a real giveaway, aren't they folks? Just like her sister Christine's."

Harry's camera moved in close to make the most of this piece of information.

"Tell me, Maureen," Spliff continued, "how long did Jessica's parents have to wait before they managed to have a child?"

Maureen felt the colour drain from her face. This wasn't what she'd anticipated at all. If she'd thought for one moment all this stuff was going to come out, she'd never have agreed to do it. Perhaps it was just a standard sort of question. "Several years," she said.

She could see that Spliff had noted her reaction instantly, and was doing a quick re-think about what he was going to say next. So it is going to be about all that, she thought. After everything I've done to keep it quiet. Oh well. I did try, Christine. I did try to follow your wishes. If I drop out they'll still do it, and I won't be around to pick up the pieces. Stick with it Maureen, she thought, Jessica's going to need you.

There was a sudden kerfuffle at the entrance, and then Sandra came in carrying a bundle of newspapers. "We're front page, early evening edition," she said. "Look everyone," and she started to hand out copies.

"Not now," said Spliff.

"But . . ."

"Not now, Sandra."

Sandra looked perplexed.

Spliff glanced meaningfully in Maureen's direction.

Sandra said, "Oh, right."

Spliff turned back to Maureen. "Would you say that Jessica was a lonely child?"

"Not noticeably," said Maureen. "She had Elspeth round to play a lot."

"You last saw Elspeth at the funeral, didn't you?"

"No, I saw her a couple of minutes ago . . ."

Spliff looked at Patsy.

"It was an accident," said Patsy.

They got onto safer territory, talking about art, and Maureen cheered up a lot. He talked quite knowledgeably about painting, which surprised her. Then he made a remark about how he couldn't personally tell a Modigliani from a Maserati, but he knew which one he'd rather have, and they were finished. Their eyes met, and suddenly she knew that he wasn't going to use any of it.

"It's about her birth, isn't it?" said Maureen.

"Partly."

"Poor Jessica," said Maureen.

"She knows it's going to be . . . unpleasant," said Spliff. "I offered her the chance to back out. She didn't take it."

Neither would I, thought Maureen, if you were asking and I was young again.

"You see," he said slowly, "I think it's about time someone spoke out about this. I'm pretty sure you feel the same way, otherwise I'd have kept my mouth shut."

The sincerity was nicely-judged. We're all in this together, sacrificing a willing victim for a higher purpose.

"I think I need a drink," she said, "and something a bit stronger than coffee. Who was it said 'I am going to drink myself dead'? Can't remember."

"Modigliani," said Spliff, smiling.

Maureen went back to her dressing room in a rather thoughtful frame of mind.

Spliff went to get a cold drink. Patsy was standing by the machine, twiddling a copper-coloured strand of hair between her fingers.

"Listen, you," said Spliff, "it's not that hard to co-ordinate things so that people don't meet up. Get your act together, will you."

"It was an accident," said Patsy.

"You're good at those, aren't you?" said Spliff. "How old is Dominic now – two and a half?"

"You bastard," said Patsy.

"That's right," said Spliff. "Don't forget it."

Harry had grabbed one of the newspapers from the bundle Sandra had brought in, although he hadn't had a chance to look at it until now. The front page had a photograph of Spliff on it, and the headline read:

Who'd Miss Missing Link?

Harry's heart sank. The piece was all about tackiness, broadcasting standards and public taste, and it was the best bit of publicity anyone could have wished for. This was your doing, wasn't it, thought Harry, looking at Spliff. You've set everything up, you haven't missed a trick. I wonder what the hell you've got planned.

Prudence went up to reception to collect her last guest. It was Jessica's old art teacher, Price the Paint. She was sitting next to Nicholas Creed and chatting away quite happily about the new Picasso exhibition; Creed had done a piece about it on the news the previous day. Prudence was impressed. She'd never spoken to Creed herself, but she was quite sure she wouldn't have been nearly as relaxed as Miss Price appeared to be. He was very good-looking, if a little elderly.

She went over and said, "Hi! I'm Prudence."

"I'll give you my personal extension Bronwyn," said Nicholas Creed. "Here," and he scribbled something on a piece of paper and handed it to her. Prudence was awestruck.

"Do you know him?" Prudence asked Bronwyn

Price, as they headed for the lift.

"No," said Bronwyn. "He's nice, isn't he?"

Prudence gulped.

Spliff glanced at his watch.

"What's up?" said Harry. "You're like a flea on a pepper-pot."

"He ought to be here by now," said Spliff.

"Who should?"

"The second-to-last piece of my jigsaw puzzle. He upped the price, the bastard, I hope he shows. Quite the little wheeler-dealer, ringing up yesterday and threatening to pull out."

"He what? You've *paid* someone to come on this programme? We pay for information, not appearances. It's expenses only. Christ, don't let Clive hear about it."

"*I* paid him, Harry," said Spliff. "And I want this one tucked away out of sight down in the basement as soon as possible. Sandra's the only one I can trust to do the job properly, and she's looking after Fern at the moment."

"Go up to reception yourself, we don't need you at the moment."

Spliff put down his clipboard. "Yeah. Good idea. See you in a minute."

Karl walked into reception as though he owned the

place. He announced himself at the desk, and looked round.

Someone went over to Spliff and tapped him on the shoulder. Spliff looked up, nodded, put down his newspaper and walked over. He was a full head shorter than Karl.

"Karl Richards?"

They didn't shake hands.

"This way."

They went over to the lift. Karl took a good look at him. Bit of a pansy, he thought. Soft. Karl himself was six foot of muscle, well-preserved for forty-eight, someone who knew how to take care of himself. He was a petty gangster this afternoon. He'd worn his Hawaiian shirt and his gold signet ring, and with all the excitement he'd forgotten to take his medication.

They travelled down to the basement. People said hello, and Spliff acknowledged them briefly. But he didn't say anything to Karl, and the two of them walked in silence until they came to a dressing room right at the end of a long corridor. Spliff unlocked the door, and they went in.

"I've been thinking . . ." said Karl.

"Well don't," said Spliff.

Karl stiffened. He hadn't liked him much over the phone, and he liked him even less in the flesh. "This is a seller's market," he said. "You're buying, and I'm selling. And I come expensive."

"We agreed a price."

"That's what I've been thinking about . . ."

"If you want to get out of here in one piece," said Spliff, "you won't wind me up any more than you've done already."

Karl smirked as Spliff counted out the notes.

"Right," said Spliff, "a girl called Sandra will be looking after you, coffee and stuff, you don't leave this room. Anything you want, you ask her."

"Is she a looker?"

"Too old for you," said Spliff. "She's twenty-eight."

Karl's eyes narrowed.

"You don't try anything with Sandra," said Spliff. "Understood?"

"Sounds like you're soft on her," said Karl. "Or wouldn't she come across for a little runt like you?"

"Have you got another shirt?" said Spliff. "The cameras can't handle too many colours at once."

Karl wasn't sure whether he'd been insulted or not. He looked at the shirt.

"I'll get Sandra to bring you another."

"Will she put it on for me?"

"No," said Spliff, "and I wouldn't advise you to ask her."

"What would you do if I did, duff me up?" said Karl, smiling.

"My duffing up is entirely verbal," said Spliff, "but I'm the best. Remember that."

Karl laughed.

"Listen," said Spliff. "I can make you look like a victim of circumstance, or I can make sure there's a lynch-mob waiting for you when you leave. Don't fuck me about. OK?"

Karl was still thinking about it as Spliff went out and shut the door behind him.

Seventeen

Sandra got Fern settled down happily with a schmaltzy video and a box of chocolates. She wasn't sure whether the chocolates were such a good idea, considering Fern's alarming ability to be sick at the slightest provocation, but she had to take her mind off everything somehow. "OK now?" she asked her.

Fern nodded.

Sandra went back up to the studio. Spliff beckoned her over.

"The man in Room 306 needs another shirt. And a bullet through the brain, whilst you're at it. You have got a phone on you, haven't you?"

Sandra shook her head. "Been a bit scatty today."

"Take mine, then." He handed it to her. "If you press hash it'll bleep me."

She nodded. "I did a rapist a couple of months back, on *Why Did He Do That?*"

"I know," said Spliff, "that's why you're doing this one."

"I hated that series," said Sandra. "Dartmoor's really grim and the interviewees kept trying to look down my blouse. What's he like then?"

"Cocky."

"Clive's going to go spare."

"Not with Potty Noodle in the audience," said Spliff.

Sandra zipped up her tracksuit, took a deep breath and knocked on the door.

"So you're Sandra," said Karl.

"I've brought you another shirt," said Sandra. "Would you like some coffee?"

"I'd love one," said Karl, slipping into his misunderstood personality. "I suppose you know why I'm here?"

Sandra nodded.

"It was a long time ago. She seduced me."

"She was fifteen."

"Some girls are women at fifteen," he said. "What were you like at that age?" He ran his eyes up and down her body.

Sandra had an overpowering urge to slap him.

"I was sorry afterwards," he added.

"Look," said Sandra, "I'm really not allowed to discuss the content of the programme with you.

Milk and sugar?"

"No milk."

When she got outside the door, she leant against the wall and breathed deeply. Maybe it was time she looked for another job. She really didn't feel up to all of this.

Spliff glanced up when she reappeared.

"I'm taking him a coffee," she said.

"Everything OK?"

"So far." Sandra sat down. "Spliff," she said, "do something for me."

"What?"

"Roast him tonight. How does he think he's going to get away with admitting to rape?"

"He did a stretch for indecent assault a couple of years after the Fern business; he reckons he's paid his dues. But he's officially better now; they needed the bed."

"You sent me down to give a clean shirt to a psychopath without telling me?"

He had the grace to look guilty.

"Can you hold all this together tonight?"

"Oh yes," said Spliff. "But it's not whether I can. It's whether I should."

She knocked and took in the coffee. Karl was standing by the mirror, the shirt open to his waist. "What do you think?" he said.

"Can't tell till it's buttoned up," said Sandra.

He started to button it, very slowly.

"Damn," he said, "old bullet wound in my hand. Can you finish it for me?"

Sandra put down the coffee and said, "The reason Spliff gave me this job is because I'm a black belt at karate."

"Pull the other one."

"If I did," said Sandra, "you wouldn't walk again." She marched to the door with the firm intention of slamming it as loudly as she could behind her.

"Last night . . ." said Prudence to Jessica.

"We went badger-watching."

"Badger-watching? Where, for goodness' sake? London Zoo?"

"Surrey. A friend of his with a farm. I slept in the spare bed, he slept on the couch."

"Gosh," said Prudence, looking relieved and surprised at the same time. "I didn't know he had a friend with a farm. What's he like? It was a he?"

"Yes," said Jessica, "Rudolph. He's very nice."

Price the Paint leant back against the sofa. There was something slightly bohemian about her, coupled with an air of sound common sense. She'd enjoyed her run-through with Spliff, although she was perfectly certain that he hadn't asked her the one question that was the whole point of her being there.

"Thank you," concluded Spliff, writing something down.

"Is that to remind you where to ask me the question you left out?"

He glanced up. "Yes."

"I was right, then? All those years ago?"

"Yes."

"I'm not sure I want to do this," said Bronwyn Price.

"It will go ahead whatever you decide. I think Jessica might want you there."

"I might as well have strings, mightn't I?" said Bronwyn, irritated. "You're not what I'd imagined at all."

"Good."

"I'm not sure that it is," said Price the Paint.

Patsy bustled over. "Message from reception," she said. "There's someone at the desk asking for you, Spliff."

"What, now?" said Spliff.

"He was very insistent. Said you wouldn't be annoyed."

"Oh, yes?" said Spliff dangerously. "And who is this person?"

"A Doctor Myers."

Spliff smiled. "Tell them to send him over."

"Have you ever heard of a Doctor Myers?" Patsy asked Prudence.

Prudence shook her head.

"I wonder what sort of a doctor he is."

"Oy, Penelope," called Spliff, beckoning to Prudence, "take Bronwyn back to her dressing room now, would you?"

Prudence looked put out.

"He only does it to annoy you," said Patsy, smiling at Prudence's pique. "Take no notice."

Rudolph had changed his jacket but that was all. "Ugh," he said as he picked his way across the cables, "how I loathe and detest these places."

"We're about to take a break," said Spliff.

"I know," said Rudolph, "I'm not a total tosser. Where can we talk?"

"We could get some sandwiches and hijack a dressing room."

"Sandwiches?" said Rudolph. "I live on bloody sandwiches."

"Can I get you a coffee?" said Patsy.

"The stuff they serve here," said Rudolph, "degrades the name of a fine and noble beverage."

"Oh," said Patsy, "you've been here before then."

"I used to present a science programme," said Rudolph. "In my youth."

"*Phylum File*," said Patsy. "I remember you now. I used to watch it when I got in from school."

"Thanks," said Rudolph. "That's all I need."

They loaded a tray with sandwiches from the machine.

"Did you have a particular dressing room in

mind?" enquired Rudolph.

Spliff smiled.

When they were alone in the lift Rudolph said, "This wasn't just a social call. I said I'd never be seen dead in this place again."

"What then?"

"DDI. I did a bit more digging for you. Here." He handed him a piece of paper.

Spliff read it. Then he smiled. "I'm glad," he said.

"I thought you would be."

Jessica and Prudence were just locking the door when Spliff and Rudolph turned the corner.

"Oh," gushed Prudence, "we were just going up to the canteen."

"Bye," said Spliff.

"Oh," said Prudence, looking at them all. "Right." She gave the key to Spliff and went.

They entered the room and sat down on the chairs. Rudolph started to dish things out. "Tuna or tuna?"

"Tuna," said Jessica.

"Tuna," said Spliff.

"Tuna," said Rudolph. "Well, that about covers that topic."

Silence.

"Well," said Rudolph, "they've discovered a new centipede in Kenya."

They all laughed. "Kenya's great," said Spliff. "I used to drive . . ."

His bleeper went off.

"Shit," said Spliff, jumping to his feet and running to the door. "Phone. Have either of you got a phone? No?" He ran out into the corridor, spotted one at the end and sprinted towards it.

"I wonder what he did with his mobile?" said Rudolph. "Oh, well."

Jessica suddenly felt as though she couldn't take any more.

"Hey," said Rudolph. He took her by the hand and led her over to the sofa, sat her down and sat down beside her. Then he put his arm round her. "You need a good hug," he said. "More than anything else in the world."

Jessica put her head on his chest and cried and cried. Spliff's unexpected appearance had shaken her and now he'd gone again. She couldn't remember ever feeling so confused about anyone in her life. She was frightened that she was going to hate him by the end of the evening, and she didn't want to.

As soon as Karl heard the knock on the door he opened it.

Spliff almost fell through. "Where is she?" he said.

"Lying down. She fainted."

Spliff strode over to the couch and leant over

Sandra, listening for her breathing and feeling her pulse at the same time. "What happened?"

"I told you, she fainted."

"What happened before that?"

"She brought me some coffee . . . look, over there on the table. Then her eyes sort of went white and she folded up. I put her on the sofa . . ."

"Give me the mobile."

Karl just stood there.

Spliff's expression darkened. "I said give it to me."

Karl gave it to him, but before he could use it Sandra opened her eyes and said, "What am I doing here?"

"You fainted," said Karl. "Remember? You were just standing there, in the middle of the floor, and you keeled over."

"Oh yes," said Sandra. "So I did."

Spliff looked surprised and sat down on the end of the couch. "And that's all that happened?"

"All?" said Sandra. "Isn't that enough?"

"Fine black-belt you turned out to be," said Spliff.

"I thought that was a wind-up," said Karl.

"No," said Spliff, "she's a killer all right." He stroked Sandra's hair. "Have you passed out like this before, Sandy?"

"Yes," said Sandra.

"Been to see anyone about it?"

"Yes," said Sandra.

"And?"

"I'm pregnant."

"You can't be."

"Oh, for goodness' sake Spliff," said Sandra, "can't you count? I'd be out here by now if it was yours."

Karl sat down heavily.

"Who's the father?" said Spliff. "Or shouldn't I ask?"

"Simon Tree."

The faint smile left Spliff's face.

"Would you like a drink of water?" asked Karl. Pregnant women didn't turn him on at all.

"Does Simon know anything about tonight's show?" asked Spliff.

"Spliff," said Sandra, "you're bullying me. I want to go home now."

"You," said Spliff to Karl, "I'm leaving you in here on your own, and I'm going to lock you in. Someone will come to get you when it's time to go up. Do you have a problem with that?"

Karl shook his head. When he forgot to take his tablets he played parts like other people changed their clothes, and the rapist was only one of many. In his Mother Teresa guise he was perfectly safe. "Go in peace, Spliff," he said. "And remember – Calcutta's a dangerous place."

"I hope to Christ he's someone else by the time we go on the air," said Spliff to Sandra, as he locked the door. "It's going to be fucking awful if he's

Ghandi."

* * *

"My life changed overnight," said Rudolph to Jessica. "It was when I was working on *Phylum File*, here, as it happens."

"You worked here as well?"

"Hmm. We were being sponsored by a chemical company. I was doing an investigation into sheep-dip. Then I got doused in the stuff, and there were some pretty shitty side-effects. The company pulled the plug on the programme. I sort of sank into nothingness for a while; then Spliff turned up one day, he'd just started *The Red Card Game*, and said let's buy a farm. So we did. I pulled myself together, and he got a nice weekend retreat. No sheep, of course. Strictly veggie, my farm."

The door opened, and Spliff reappeared.

Eighteen

"What was all that bleepy business about?" said Rudolph, keeping his arm firmly round Jessica.

Spliff looked at the arm with some disapproval. "Sandra fainted," he said. "She's pregnant."

Rudolph's eyes widened.

"Not guilty," said Spliff. "It was Simon Tree."

"Ah," said Rudolph.

"Ah indeed," said Spliff. Then he remembered – "Oh Christ. Now Sandra's gone I haven't got . . ." He broke off.

"I think we'd better change the subject," said Rudolph.

"I refuse to talk about centipedes," said Spliff, "or any other invertebrates, for that matter." He went over to the bench. "The tea's cold," he added irritably.

"Well, *I* need another one," said Rudolph, "anyone else?"

The other two nodded. Rudolph slowly disentangled himself from Jessica and went.

Spliff sat down. "I don't want you getting ideas that I'm going to be soft on you," he said. "I'm paid to hurt people."

"I know," she said.

"I'm not sure that you do." He put his hands behind his head, leant back in the chair and stretched out his legs. "Tell me a story."

"All right," said Jessica. "Once upon a time there was an owl. Owl met lots of other birds in the forest, but she had never met another owl. Then one day she saw a strange bird sitting on a tree by a lake. She flew down and sat beside him and she could see that their reflections in the water were almost identical. But she didn't know which was real – the owl or his reflection. And then a gust of wind blew across the surface of the lake and the reflection broke into a thousand pieces."

"But when the wind had gone the reflection came back again," said Spliff, "and it was very entertaining to watch. You get more range in a reflection than you do in the real thing."

"But no blood or guts or heart."

"That was a nice story," said Spliff. "Don't spoil it with offal."

She laughed. Then the conversation seemed to flag and they just looked at one another. "Draw me," said Spliff softly. He handed her his clipboard and gave her his pen. "Turn to the last page. It's blank."

"Is it?"

"It's always blank. We have to believe that. Whatever our genes, whatever our upbringing, in the end it is down to us. We can tear some pages out, or scribble on top of what's already written. But most of the pages are blank."

Jessica started to draw, tentatively at first, then with more assurance. She began to lose herself in the drawing, feeling his face with the pen.

She shaded his hair, darkening it a little at a time, altering the pressure here and there, following the form. She glanced up and saw that he was watching her hand. He raised his eyes, and for a moment it was as though the paper was some sort of intermediary, and they had touched. She reached his mouth, and he smiled. She moved on quickly to his ear. He scratched it. Was any part of him safe? She smudged in some dark around his eyes and he blinked. She leant back and studied the result. It was very like him.

He took the clipboard from her, looked at the drawing for a long time and then handed it back to her. "It's a terrific piece of work for an owl," he said. "Sign it."

She signed it.

"I'm going to have to go in a moment."

"I know."

"I won't see you again until the show."

"I know."

"That owl," said Spliff, "if she ever needs anything, all she has to do is hoot."

Jessica smiled.

"You know how to hoot, don't you?" said Spliff. "Just put your lips together and blow."

Rudolph opened the door.

"Gotta go," said Spliff. He stood in the doorway for a moment, looking at her. Then without saying anything further, he went.

"I want you to remember something this evening," said Rudolph gently. "Spliff will make no allowances once the programme starts, not for anyone. The moment he's in front of a camera he's the complete professional. Don't expect anything else."

"Prudence," said Spliff. "Sandra's ill, you're going to have to look after Fern."

Prudence's eyes widened. "But she's the other main guest."

"Oh come on, Prudence, you can do it. Just think before you speak." He started to walk away.

"Oh!" said Prudence. "I forgot. There's a little gathering in room twenty. Potty Noodle's there; they've all been discussing the piece in the paper." ·

"Listen, Prudence," said Spliff. "I've got a surprise guest in Room 306. Clive doesn't know about him, he needs to be brought up and kept apart from Fern. I want it kept quiet. And I want you to get a bloke to do it. Get Bruce or someone, anyone. But you're not to do it, understand? I want him brought on at this point in the programme . . ." He grabbed her clipboard and wrote down the timing. "OK?"

She nodded.

"Good girl." He hurried off down the corridor. At the end of it he turned and blew her a kiss. Prudence perked up no end.

"I like to think of *Missing Link* as the new drama," said Strickland. "No expensive sets, no actors to pay . . ."

Spliff walked in, and poured himself an orange juice.

Simon Tree said, "Hello Spliff. Good to see you again. Thought I'd come along to see the first show of the new era." His voice oozed insincerity the way a cane toad's skin oozes poison.

"I don't know whether you're aware of it," said Spliff, "but Sandra didn't feel well. She's gone home."

Strickland smiled, and looked at Tree. "Sandra?"

"She fainted," said Spliff. "And the reason she fainted . . ."

"I've just remembered I've got to make a phone call and there's no coverage in here," interrupted Simon Tree, getting out his mobile. "Sorry about this. Won't be long."

As he passed, Spliff caught him by the sleeve and said under his breath, "Strickland likes your wife. I can make your relationship with Sandra sound very tacky indeed. I'm going to ring Sandra in half an hour, and you'd better be there . . ."

Tree gave Spliff a look of pure venom, before leaving.

"So, Spliff, nice bit of publicity for you today, wasn't it?" said Strickland.

"Very nice," said Spliff.

He held up a newspaper. "*Voyeuristic, tasteless, titillating, sensationalist, exploitative* . . . You've done great things with this programme."

"We've got a cracker lined up tonight," said Clive.

"Don't tell me any details," said Strickland. "The whole point of this show is its surprises."

"I really must be off now," said Spliff. "Things to do, people to screw, you know how it is."

He left.

"You have to give a man like Spliff his head, don't you?" said Strickland.

Clive felt the programme beginning to slip away from him.

Patsy was outside, scanning the queue for Eveline. She had telephoned her, saying she'd been selected at random to be offered a ticket for *Missing Link*; they wanted a representative audience, not just people who'd written in. All expenses paid, naturally.

Patsy glanced at her watch, and then suddenly she saw her, a slim middle-aged woman with a sharp little nose that reminded her of the beak of a hummingbird. Patsy walked briskly over to her, tapped her on the shoulder, revealed her identity tag and said, "Eveline Marshall? Hi. My name's Patsy. I'm a researcher on *Missing Link* and we'd like you to appear on it. Only for a couple of minutes. Is that all right?"

Eveline looked thunderstruck.

The woman in front of Eveline in the queue said, "I'd do it. Like a shot. Go on love, you'll regret it if you don't."

"What's the programme about?"

Patsy laughed. "I can't say that, can I? But your bit is just something to do with your job. Why don't you come with me and meet Spliff; he'll convince you."

Eveline looked relieved at the mention of the job connection. The woman in front of her was quite blatantly consumed with envy.

"All right," said Eveline.

"We just need to get you to sign a little form . . ." said Patsy, as they went inside. "Won't take a tick."

Spliff looked up.

"This is Eveline," said Patsy. She was standing behind Eveline, so when she waved the consent form at Spliff, Eveline didn't see.

"Oh good," said Spliff. "Nice to meet you, Eveline." He smiled. All of a sudden there was something of the little boy about him.

"Patsy said it was something about my job," said Eveline, with a couple of birdlike movements of the head.

"That's right," said Spliff cheerfully. "Although anything can happen on *Missing Link*."

Eveline wondered who had been misbehaving themselves at work. Not her, not these days. She'd joined AA several years ago now, and life was looking up – as long as she didn't get a phone call from Fern. Those always wound her up. Spliff smiled at her again, and she felt quite maternal. Maybe if Fern had been a boy things would have been different.

"God almighty, Prudence, I could wring your neck sometimes!" shouted Spliff. He pushed her into the make-up room.

"But I just thought . . . he'd been down there for ages without anything to drink. So I took him a coffee."

"And you got a nasty surprise. It bloody well serves you right. Why can't you just do as you're told. The man is a nutter, that's why I wanted a bloke to bring him up."

"I didn't bring him up, it's not time."

"I know that! But you went in there, spreading your idea of sunshine and some psychopath's idea of coffee to a man who was communing with God. Fucking hell Prudence, how on earth did you ever get a degree in Media Studies?"

Prudence looked indignant. "I got a two-one. It was all right though, Spliff. I mean, he's quite happy waiting down there. I just thought I ought to tell you he isn't wearing anything except his underpants and he's praying to a rubbish bin. That's all."

Spliff laughed suddenly. "Go and get Rudolph."

"Oh gosh, yes, of course, Rudolph's a doctor isn't he? You're not cross any more?"

"No, Prunella, I'm not cross. You've had a lot on your plate today."

Rudolph looked at Spliff in disbelief. "You want me to go down there and convince the son of the west wind that he's a suburban rapist?"

"That's right," said Spliff, not looking up from the notes he was reading.

"I'm not a fucking psychiatrist."

Spliff looked up. "Help me out, Rudolph. You've been there."

"You really know how to flatter a guy, don't you?"

"You're good at all that arm-round-the-shoulder stuff. And besides, I haven't got the time." He glanced at the clock. "I want the Karl Richards that seduced Fern. I *need* him."

"You don't want much."

"Get him remembering things. Take him back. Oh, and hide the rubbish bin."

Nineteen

"Sandra? Let me speak to the shit."

"He's in the bathroom," said Sandra.

There was a click as Spliff hung up. Sandra looked at the receiver as though it had bitten her. All she'd had from Simon was a bloody phone call, asking her to tell Spliff he was in the bathroom when the little bastard rang. He'd only asked her how she was as an afterthought.

* * *

Karl opened the door of the dressing room fully clothed, and looking perfectly normal. "You're the person who's come to collect me?" he queried. "I thought it wasn't for another hour."

"It isn't," said Rudolph, "I've just come to keep you company for a bit." Apart from the fact that the rubbish bin was sitting in a position of prominence on the sink, nothing was untoward. Rudolph sat down, and Karl followed suit.

"My name's Doctor Myers," said Rudolph.

"Ah," said Karl.

"Do you know why you're here, Karl?"

"Of course. They're going to interview me about my latest invention."

This was a new slant. "Tell me about it," said Rudolph.

"Well," said Karl, "you know kitchen knives?"

Rudolph nodded. This sounded promising.

"I've found a way of storing them. A strip of magnetic metal on the wall."

Rudolph sighed; it was going to be a long hard slog. "Have you ever used a knife on anyone, Karl?"

"It's not a very violent profession, being an inventor."

"No," said Rudolph, "I don't suppose it is. Listen Karl, will you do something for me? I want you to think back, to twenty-three years ago. You were living with a woman called Eveline . . ." He lifted down the rubbish bin and hid it under the sink. "She had a daughter. Fern."

"I don't know . . ." said Karl. His brows drew together slightly, and Rudolph could see a muscle in his jaw working. Karl was pretty muscular altogether. Although Rudolph was tall he was very slight; he didn't fancy his chances against Karl in the least if it came to anything.

"You did a deal," said Rudolph, "with Spliff. He's paying you to tell us what you did to Fern. You sewed him up nicely you know, you must be quite the wheeler-dealer."

Karl looked confused for a moment.

"Tell me," said Rudolph, "do you gangsters carry guns or knives?"

Karl's eyes narrowed and his whole demeanour changed. "What's it to you?" he asked suspiciously.

Christ, thought Rudolph, that was one of the quickest character flips I've ever seen. The man's a walking thesis. "Just asking," said Rudolph.

"Well don't," said Karl. "Or I might be forced to show it to you."

Rudolph found his eyes travelling across Karl's jacket and trousers, looking for bulges.

"Something wrong with my jacket?" snapped Karl.

"No, no," said Rudolph. He realised he was sweating. "I just wondered if you were as hot as I am. Tell me, did you come through security with Spliff?"

"Uh huh."

Rudolph felt a little bit better. If Karl had been carrying anything nasty surely they'd have stopped him. On the other hand, the security staff were cheap labour from Albania, and they buggered off to college as soon as they'd fiddled the required paperwork. Rudolph wished his heart would stop hammering. It couldn't be good for it. Then he had a sudden thought. "Karl," he said, "are you on any medication?"

Karl looked thoughtful, as though the word *medication* might have some mystical interpretation.

That's it, thought Rudolph, he's on tablets and he's forgotten to take them. The perspiration was making him feel clammy and uncomfortable, and it wasn't a sensation that contributed all that much towards concentrating on the problem in hand. "It really is awfully hot in here," said Rudolph. "Think I'll take my jacket off." He lifted his arm, and realised too late that it looked as though he was going for a weapon.

"No you don't," said Karl, moving fast, "hold it right there."

And Karl did have a knife, after all. Rudolph started to think very quickly. Spliff wouldn't be coming to get him. By the time Spliff realised what had happened he'd be halfway through *Missing Link*. Rudolph felt a bit peeved. He'd have to get out of this on his own.

"Nice knife," said Rudolph.

"Shut up," said Karl, "because I *am* going to let you take your jacket off. Slowly."

Rudolph took off his jacket.

"Your shirt."

Rudolph complied.

"Trousers."

Shit, thought Rudolph. He took off his trousers.

Karl held the knife against Rudolph's neck with one hand, and shook the clothes with the other. A shower of oddments fell onto the floor.

Rudolph was really frightened now. There was an intensity about the man that hadn't been there before, his mouth was set and his hands shook very slightly, as though he was trying to contain something.

"Get dressed."

Rudolph got dressed again with a feeling of relief. He was never at his best in just his underpants.

"We're right down the end of the corridor here," said Karl, "so it's not worth yelling. I wouldn't try it. It might upset me."

Rudolph lifted his hands as though that was the last thing that had been on his mind. He had a horror of being gagged.

"You won't get the money back," said Karl. "It's in my pocket."

"He gave you some money? I'll believe it when I see it. Spliff diddles everyone."

Karl put one hand into his pocket and pulled out a selection of objects which he placed on the coffee table. Keys, coins, toothpicks, pieces of paper . . . And at long last, a small bottle of tablets. He looked at the tablets as though he ought to know what they were, but he couldn't quite figure it out.

"Shouldn't you take one of those?" said Rudolph gently.

"You're right," said Karl. "Thanks." He opened the bottle and swallowed one of the tablets, then he put his hand back in his pocket and pulled out a bundle of notes. "See?" he said.

"I'm impressed," said Rudolph. With any luck it was just a matter of time now. He glanced at the clock. It was twenty-five to nine.

"They're sending someone down to get me," said Karl.

"Get you in what sense?" said Rudolph warily.

"Don't play games with me," said Karl.

"That someone," said Rudolph, "is me."

"And I'm Mother Teresa," growled Karl.

If only, thought Rudolph. Try it. "I'm a great admirer of the work you do in Calcutta, Mother . . ." he started.

Karl transferred the knife to his other hand and hit Rudolph across the face.

Jessica saw Spliff walk into the studio from the other side. He was dressed entirely in black.

"There's Potty Noodle," said Prudence, "over there. Oh! Shouldn't have let that one slip out, should I? I don't get it though, I don't see how you get 'Potty Noodle' out of Strickland . . . And that's Simon Tree, I didn't expect to see him here. I wouldn't have spotted him if it wasn't for his wife, see, the one with the face like an aardvark . . . shouldn't say that really should I, but she's a prize bitch . . . Oh and look, there's Nicholas Creed, the newsreader . . ."

Jessica wished she could just tell Prudence to shut up. She saw Spliff nod one last time to someone, and glance round; then the theme-tune started, and the title sequence unrolled on the screen at the back. Spliff walked out onto the set, smiling at the whistles and the applause of the crowd.

Twenty

Spliff sat down and raised a hand. The applause died away. He grinned impishly. "Hello, everyone. It's Saturday the twenty-seventh of June, the year's 2020, and England have been drawn against Karetsefia. Welcome to this edition of *Missing Link*, the investigative chatshow, and the last one of the series. My name's Spliff, and this week I think we're going to get everything, laughter, tears, reunions, old wounds, lots of surprises . . . You know the form – two subjects who've never met, their life histories, and an unexpected tie-in at the end. And so, without further ado, let's meet our first subject, Jessica Pierce, a student from Kingston upon Thames . . ."

Prudence gave Jessica a little push in the small of her back; the jingle started, and she walked down the steps. Their eyes met. His were completely expressionless. She sat down on the sofa.

"Say hello to the viewers, Jessica."

She said hello.

"So, Jessica," said Spliff, "you've absolutely no idea why you're here, have you?"

She wanted to laugh. Instead she shook her head. It would be all right. Just follow his lead.

"Then let's get started. We'll begin in 1998, the year of your birth . . ."

The Cedars appeared obligingly on the screen behind them. She couldn't see the audience very well at all, it was a relief really. The lights were much hotter than they'd been during the run-through, and the chrysanthemums had responded by pumping out their distinctive Christmassy smell. She suddenly remembered that Spliff's mother had grown white chrysanthemums. Had she grown lumps and bumps and bunions too?

"Let's hear a bit about your childhood, Jessica. You lived in a private village, didn't you? Security guards, electronic gates, broken glass on the top of the walls . . ."

"You make it sound like a prison," said Jessica, as though she were reading a script inside her head. "It wasn't. I had a very happy childhood."

"But lonely."

"Not really."

He switched to the churchyard story. The whole thing was like a medieval dance; very intricate, very precise, his feet, her feet, he led, she followed. The pauses, the timing, the witty little asides, the conspiratorial grin. She realised how good he really was. Yesterday had been nothing.

She strolled through the medical room incident at school; she got a laugh from the audience, and she felt it go to her head like champagne. There was a slight smile on Spliff's face; he'd noticed. She felt surprisingly relaxed and cheerful – how quickly she'd forgotten this was the lead-up to something else.

"You said you weren't a lonely child," said Spliff. "I think you're lying."

It was as if he'd pulled a string. She froze again, right on cue.

"You got a life from books," said Spliff. "The same as me. I was an only child as well, Jessica. And I loathed every minute. Now I'd like to talk about your mother for a bit." The picture of Christine Pierce appeared on the screen. "How old was she when you were born?"

The exchange went exactly as before, until they got to the part where Spliff said, ". . . your mother might not have been who she said she was at all . . ."

"What exactly do you mean?" said Jessica.

"I don't mean she had a secret identity," said Spliff, smiling artfully at the camera. "But before we go into that I want to talk about your father. You got along better with him than you did with your mother, didn't you?"

"Yes."

"Do you think that's because you looked like him, and not your mother?" He didn't wait for her to answer. "Tell us a bit about him."

She talked a bit about him.

"How old was your father when you were born?"

"A bit older than my mother, maybe."

"You never knew his exact age either? But you think he was – oh – late forties when you were born?"

She shrugged. "I suppose so."

"He was sixty."

"What?"

"When you were born, he was sixty. He had a lot more years to account for than those he told you about. You said he was an antiques dealer. What did he do before that?"

No allowances. She could hear Rudolph's words ringing in her ears. No allowances; once he's in front of the camera he's the complete professional. Don't expect anything else.

"I know he did a Chemistry degree," said Jessica.

"He was employed as a research chemist by DDI." Once again Spliff looked at the camera as though this was quite a laugh. "We'll come back to DDI later, too. Oh what a tangled web we weave tonight."

Jessica's earlier euphoria had completely gone now.

Spliff turned towards her again. "If I mentioned Suzannah or Laura . . ."

She shook her head. "They don't mean a thing."

"They meant quite a lot to your father, I think.

Suzannah was his first wife, Laura was his second and your mother was his third."

She knew the camera was on her face, she saw the little red light come on.

"There were a fair number of mistresses, as well. Svetlana, Zoë . . ."

"Elspeth's mother?"

"Yes."

It was hard to assimilate that one. Her father and Zoë . . .

"I want to make it clear to you Jessica," said Spliff, "that these women were all before he met your mother."

She managed to remain expressionless, but her mind was racing. This snippet was no big deal for him, this came early on in the programme, this was just for hors d'oeuvres. The camera was still on her. There was an expectant hush. They were all waiting for her reaction.

"Oh, well," she said flippantly, "lots of men sleep around before they meet the right partner."

Harry's camera came on. Spliff winked at the camera and grinned and the audience laughed. Damn you, she thought, I know you're using me but I didn't expect it to feel like this.

"I'd have thought there was one question you'd want to ask immediately," said Spliff, serious again.

What question? She couldn't think of any question. Her mind blanked.

"With two marriages behind him, Jessica, the question we're all asking is – did Edward Pierce father any other children?"

Her light came on. She still couldn't think of anything to say.

"Both Suzannah and Laura married a second time, and both of them had children the second time round. The obvious conclusion would be that Edward Pierce was infertile – if it weren't for Jessica. We're going to bring on Jessica's childhood friend now – Elspeth Black."

The jingle started up again, and Elspeth minced down the steps; her dress was too tight for her to do anything else. The audience clapped. She grinned at Jessica.

Jessica smiled back; it was an effort. She moved along the sofa to let Elspeth sit nearest to Spliff.

"So, Elspeth," said Spliff, "you've known Jessica for most of your life, haven't you?"

"Ever since we used to shout rude words at the paper boy." She giggled.

Thanks Elspeth, thought Jessica.

Elspeth started to talk, punctuating what she said with giggles. When a bit about a plastic crocodile came up she kept looking at Spliff as though he ought to know why the word crocodile was so emotive.

"She finds crocodiles a turn-on," said Spliff. "All those gently smiling jaws."

Elspeth shrieked with laughter, and Jessica

decided that perhaps she'd been friends with Elspeth for long enough. Some people change. Others don't.

Elspeth finished a rather silly story about a paddling pool, and Spliff leant back in his chair and smiled at her. She seemed to melt like cheese in front of him. "The painting Jessica gave you for your eighteenth birthday present was a bit special, wasn't it?"

An electronic reproduction of the painting in question came up on the screen. Jessica wilted.

"I want you all to take a good look at this," said Spliff, "because it's going to be important later."

"It's the self-portrait I asked her to do," said Elspeth.

Jessica could have died. What she'd been capable of doing at eighteen wasn't a patch on what she could do now. It wasn't even a very good likeness. It looked like . . . oh God, that was ridiculous. It looked exactly like a younger version of the woman she'd seen on the first morning, the one with the appalling haircut, the one who'd averted her eyes. *That* was why the woman's face had seemed so familiar.

"Thank you, Elspeth," said Spliff.

Twenty-one

Spliff was saying something, and she was drifting; *concentrate.*

"And so we've got someone who knows a bit about it . . . her old art teacher, Bronwyn Price."

Jessica gave an inward sigh of relief. Thank God there was going to be a good one. The jingle started up and Price the Paint came down the steps, a wary smile on her face. They hugged one another, a sort of mutual moral support signal.

Spliff grinned disarmingly. "Bronwyn. You've been teaching art for eighteen years. How good would you say Jessica was?"

"Oh, she's very good," said Bronwyn, without hesitation. "You didn't do her any favours showing that self-portrait."

"I know," said Spliff, "let's rectify it." He turned to the screen on his left, and a beautiful watercolour of some marguerites appeared.

Good choice, thought Bronwyn, I wonder who selected it.

The flowers were lying scattered on a doorstep, caught in a shaft of sunlight, and the treatment was very free and loose. "Impressive stuff," said Spliff. He flicked over a page on his clipboard.

Bronwyn caught a glimpse of something, a pencil sketch, she couldn't see all of it – but she could see the signature. He smiled at her, and she knew he'd done it deliberately. She looked more closely at him, the way she would if she was going to paint him. He wasn't very easy to read.

"You met Jessica's parents on open evenings, didn't you," said Spliff. "We've already heard about one of those." The audience laughed, remembering. "What did you make of them?"

"Pleasant."

He gave her an old-fashioned look off-camera. "Go on."

She hesitated. What did he expect her to say? They weren't even a third of the way through the programme. She decided not to answer.

He pushed again. "Were they different in any way from the other parents?"

"They were older."

"How do you feel about older parents, Bronwyn? As a teacher?"

"Well . . . they're good about things like dental appointments and music lessons. They generally have more money. And they have a whole host of varied experiences to pass on."

"And the downside?"

"They've often forgotten what it's like to be children. They're over-protective. They don't have friends with children the same age. They get ill. And they sometimes die."

"So," said Spliff, "in balance . . . older parents . . . good thing or bad thing?"

"Well . . . bad, really, I suppose," said Bronwyn. "Particularly if the child is an only child."

"Jessica?" Spliff turned to her.

"I don't know," said Jessica.

"You're only twenty-two, and you have no other living relatives apart from an aunt. How do you feel about that?"

"Bloody annoyed," Jessica found herself saying, rather unexpectedly.

"I think we can take that as a vote for bad then, can we?" said Spliff.

"What about your vote?"

"My vote," said Spliff. "I don't know if I'm allowed a vote." He looked at the audience. "What do you think?"

Naturally they all chorused a *yes*.

"Bad, then," said Spliff.

"We've given you the reasons for our answers," said Price the Paint. "What about yours?"

"My father died when I was six," said Spliff, "and my mother died when I was seventeen. They were older parents too, and I was an only child."

Bronwyn looked from one to the other. "You've got a lot in common then, haven't you?"

"Yes," said Spliff, "we have."

Bronwyn's eyes fastened on the clipboard again. The pencil drawing was a portrait of Spliff. She felt as though she was missing something important.

"The question of whether to have a child is the most important decision most of us ever make," Spliff was saying. "We owe it to those unborn children to take that decision as wisely as possible. Thank you for joining us, Price the Paint."

She smiled and stood up. She'd got off lightly. She gave Jessica a peck on the cheek, and as she turned to leave she saw Spliff and Jessica glance at one another. It was the sort of look that passes between people who know one another extremely well. Feeling very uneasy, Bronwyn went and sat in the audience to watch the rest of the show. Someone tapped her hesitantly on the shoulder.

"Seems silly not to join you," whispered a beautifully-modulated voice. "If you don't mind, that is."

"My pleasure," said Bronwyn, and she moved up a seat to make room for Nicholas Creed.

"You can't be sick *again*," said Prudence, glancing at the clock. "There can't be anything left." She'd just delivered Maureen safely upstairs; things hadn't been going too badly, considering she was dealing with one extra charge. Until now.

Fern shook her head miserably. "There isn't anything left," she said. "And all that lovely make-up Louise-Marie did . . ."

"Don't worry. Louise-Marie can touch up anything at a moment's notice."

Fern laughed.

Prudence said, "What did I say? Oh!" And then she laughed as well.

Louise-Marie was leaning against the make-up counter, watching the programme on a monitor.

"Fern needs a face-repair," said Prudence.

"No problem," said the French girl.

Prudence went over to watch the monitor. "How's it been going?" she enquired.

"Good," said Louise-Marie, quickly massaging a squirt of foundation into Fern's skin. "Bit more depth than usual. But he isn't sticking to the script. I bet Clive's shitting himself."

Fern turned her head to look. Jessica's self-portrait had just come up on the screen. "Hey," said Fern, "that's me!"

"*Merde*," said Louise-Marie, "she shouldn't be watching this."

Prudence jumped up and switched off the monitor.

Fern looked disappointed.

"You can't," said Prudence, "it's not allowed.

Oh God! Spliff asked me to do something, and I forgot."

"Asked you to do what?"

"I can't say," said Prudence.

"Oh, he's going to deviate from the script even more, is he?" said Louise-Marie. "I thought as much."

"Why?"

"*Everyone's* here. Potty Noodle, some TV critics, an MP, Nicholas Creed . . ."

"Oh God," said Prudence again, "how could I forget?"

"Well, why don't you go and do whatever it is you're meant to do," said Louise-Marie, "and I'll push Fern on when she's cued."

"What about Jessica?"

"Who's Jessica?" asked Fern.

"Oh, *hell*," said Prudence.

"I'll deal with her," said Louise-Marie. "Now scarper, before you drop any more bricks."

Spliff stood up as Maureen Garvey came down the steps, and he joined in the applause. It took her a little while – she wasn't too good at steps these days – but there weren't very many of them. She sat down next to Spliff, with Jessica on her left.

"Maureen Garvey, Christine's sister and Jessica's aunt," said Spliff, "and the only relative she seems to have left. How old are you, Miss Garvey, if that isn't a terribly impertinent question?"

"Seventy-five."

"So you were born in . . ." he flicked his fingers, "1947 . . . 6."

"Five," said Maureen.

"Five," said Spliff. "1945." He grinned. "Never was much cop at maths."

Like hell, thought Maureen.

"And you were Christine's *younger* sister."

And he'd got her, just like that. She felt such a fool.

"How much younger?" said Spliff.

"Five years." Maureen felt the situation close round her. It wasn't going to be about Jessica's pictures at all, was it?

"So that makes Christine Pierce . . . what . . . born in 1940 . . . help me out, Maureen . . ." There was some patchy laughter from the audience.

"Fifty-eight years old when Jessica was born," said Maureen quietly.

There was complete silence. Fifty-eight. The more Jessica said the figures in her head the sillier they sounded, like a nursery rhyme.

"You promised your sister you'd take care of all the paperwork at Edward's funeral so that Jessica would never find out, didn't you?" said Spliff to Maureen. "And you kept your promise."

Maureen didn't say anything.

"So maybe we've been barking up the wrong tree here," said Spliff. "We've all been assuming there

was something a bit dubious about Jessica's father
– no children in his first two marriages, remember
– but perhaps it ought to be Jessica's *mother* we're
querying."

Maureen just looked at him, stony-faced.

"It would be fair to say that Jessica takes more
after her father, wouldn't it?"

"You know it would," said Maureen sharply.

She saw him mentally take a pace back.

"Let's clear up the matter of Jessica's father
first then, so that we can rule him out of the equation if
necessary."

"I thought maths wasn't your thing," said
Maureen.

Spliff smiled the way he always smiled when
someone got one over on him – with real pleasure.
"This little problem about whether Edward Pierce was
capable of fathering children . . ." he said. "What do
you remember about Eveline?"

"Eveline?" said Maureen. "I never met her."

"No, but Christine talked to you about her,
didn't she?"

"Eveline was ancient history."

"Tell us anyway."

Spliff glanced at Jessica. Jessica was pale, and
sitting very still. She rallied slightly as he caught her
eye and something unspoken seemed to pass between
them. Curious, thought Maureen. They almost seem to
be allies.

Twenty-two

"Edward Pierce was working at DDI when he met Eveline. Just to remind you folks at home, DDI is the pharmaceutical company that makes the cancer vaccine. They've made billions out of it because it's not cheap, is it? That little jab costs a lot of money. They also made *Parfromol*, the migraine drug that was withdrawn when it came to light that the trial results had been falsified. Tell me, Maureen, would it be true to say that out of all Edward Pierce's previous attachments, the one his wife resented the most was Eveline?"

"I suppose so."

"What do you know about her?"

"She was an administrator of some sort."

"Smart? Chic, even? Clever?"

"Yes. But she liked a drink, I think she had a bit of a problem in that area."

"Eveline tried to blow the whistle on DDI,"

said Spliff, "and she lost her job as a result. Edward Pierce lost his eleven years later, when everything came out."

It's all going to be bad, thought Jessica. All of it.

"It now looks as though," said Spliff, turning to the sheet of paper that Rudolph had given him, "Edward Pierce was set up to take the rap for someone else."

"Oh, yes?" said Maureen. She'd always liked Edward.

"When Eveline told him the results had been tampered with he tried to check, but by then someone had destroyed the evidence. He didn't believe her; she didn't believe him. She left the country. Eleven years later Edward Pierce became the fall-guy, only to be exonerated by later evidence. But that would be another programme entirely."

"So he was innocent," said Maureen. "Good."

Jessica tried to keep her thoughts in order. A moment ago her father had been a bad guy; now he was a good guy again.

"Why did Eveline really leave the country, I wonder?" said Spliff casually.

"I think you know why," said Maureen.

Spliff just looked at her, waiting for her to go on.

"She was pregnant," said Maureen.

There was a long pause.

"When are we talking about here . . ." said

Spliff. "1982? Edward was forty-five."

"Damn his age," said Maureen sharply, "I think it ought to be made clear immediately that Eveline had the pregnancy terminated. Otherwise Jessica could be thinking all sorts of things."

"A termination was Edward's idea, wasn't it?" said Spliff.

"He never wanted children," said Maureen. "Not when he was younger."

"So why did he decide to have Jessica?"

"People do change," said Maureen. "*Memento mori*, perhaps."

"I think you'll have to translate that for me, Maureen," said Spliff.

"Remember we must die," said Maureen. "And I'm quite sure you didn't need *me* to tell you."

"I did duffing up at school," said Spliff, "not Greek."

"Latin," corrected Maureen.

Spliff shrugged and grinned and Maureen felt annoyed with herself for getting caught again.

He turned back to Harry's camera. "So," he said, "we have now established that Edward Pierce was capable of fathering children. But what happened to Eveline? How did Eveline's life turn out?"

"I don't see the relevance," said Maureen.

Jessica could see Spliff was watching the clock.

"The reason it's relevant," said Spliff, "is because Eveline didn't have an abortion at all. She went to France and had the baby, returning to England a few years later. Our next guest after the break is Edward and Eveline's daughter, folks. Jessica's half-sister, Fern. Only Fern doesn't know that yet. Stay with us."

The red light on Harry's camera went off, the audience stirred and then began to chatter. "Three minutes," said Clive.

Louise-Marie was there almost instantly saying, "Come on Jessica, you and Maureen have to go off now."

"OK," said Clive to Spliff, "I'm not stupid. I realise you're doing your own thing this evening. Strickland thinks it's great so far, nice new sister for poor orphan Jessica; I'm the fucking producer and I don't even know the tie-in."

"That's a knotty one for you," said Spliff.

"You don't have to go all the way back to your dressing room," said Louise-Marie to Jessica. "It's hardly worth it anyway. Stay in the make-up room with me if you like. You go on again in fifteen minutes."

"Has anyone ever just legged it?"

"No," said Louise-Marie, "but we did have a punch-up during a commercial break once. And sod Spliff's orders, you could do with a bit of blusher."

Jessica sat in the chair as Louise-Marie dabbed

at her face.

"Do you hate him yet?" asked Louise-Marie.

Jessica didn't say anything.

"He's doing a job," said Louise-Marie. "He does this sort of thing with lots of people, makes them feel special; lulls them into a false sense of security for maximum emotional impact and then goes for the jugular. Good television."

"Is it?" said Jessica.

"Cheer up," said Louise-Marie, "you never know. This half-sister might be really nice. He's going to give her a fairly awful time of it, actually. Worse than he gave you."

A half-sister. It sounded silly, as though someone had split her in two like a blade of grass with their thumbnail. Spliff probably knew as much about Fern as he did about Jessica. Jessica was only one out of the dozens of guests he had in a year. She'd known the man for two days; was that really enough time to say *this relationship is something special? Something important?*

"He never gets close to anyone," said Louise-Marie, as if Jessica had spoken aloud. "Believe me, I tried. He doesn't mix with any of us when he's not working. And as soon as he's got time off he goes abroad."

"Kenya."

"Yes," said Louise-Marie, surprised. "He's got friends there. You seem to know an awful lot about him."

Jessica shrugged.

"I hope it's occurred to you," said Louise-Marie, annoyed that Jessica didn't seem inclined to talk, "that he might have been making a special effort to win you over so that you *really* crack up when the time comes."

Prudence appeared in the doorway. "I got hold of Bruce," she said, "he's gone to get Spliff's mystery man. And you-know-who's on now. She was sick again."

Louise-Marie glared at her.

"Oh, lighten up Louise-Marie," said Prudence, "I didn't give anything away."

Bruce glanced at his watch, and knocked on the door a second time. He tried the handle, but the door was locked. Perhaps the guy's had a heart attack, he thought, and he kicked in the door with his foot.

There was a man sitting tied to a chair, gagged. Another man lay on the couch, fast asleep. What was going on? Which one was the one Spliff wanted?

The man on the couch stirred, roused by the sound of Bruce's entrance. The man in the chair looked wild-eyed and desperate, but he would, wouldn't he, thought Bruce. Which one's the nutter? "I've come to collect Karl Richards," said Bruce. He couldn't think of anything else to say.

The man on the sofa sat up and rubbed his eyes.

"Which one of you is Karl?" said Bruce again.

Karl looked confused.

"Why is that man wearing a gag?" asked Bruce.

"Search me," said Karl.

Bruce went over to Rudolph and undid the gag. Rudolph took a deep breath, as though he'd been underwater for a long time. "Who are you?" said Bruce.

"Doctor Rudolph Myers," said Rudolph. "Would you be so good as to untie me?"

Bruce looked from Karl to Rudolph and back again.

"Don't ask me," said Karl. "Never seen the bugger before."

"And your name?" said Bruce.

"Karl Richards."

Bruce untied Rudolph immediately. There was blood on the Hawaiian shirt that had been used to gag him.

Rudolph grimaced, stretched himself and rubbed his wrists. Then he glanced at his watch and said, "Get him up to Spliff will you, you've only got five minutes. He's OK now, he's taken his medication."

"What about you?"

"I'll be all right," said Rudolph.

Bruce left with Karl, although he didn't look frightfully happy about it.

Rudolph washed his face and tried to make

himself look presentable again. The whole business had dredged up unpleasant memories from school when someone had tied him to a tree and gagged him, and then used the space round him on the trunk for archery practice. He'd never been able to listen to the *William Tell Overture* since. He peered at himself in the mirror. He thought he looked old today, and the thought depressed him. Most of the time he liked living alone, but once in a while he wished he could find someone other than a chat show host to keep him company at weekends. Preferably someone who could cook a really good *gigot à la provençale*.

They wouldn't let him back into the studio until the next commercial break, so Rudolph sat down on the floor in the corridor outside and waited.

Twenty-three

"Welcome back after the break," said Spliff. "It's now time to introduce you to our second guest, Fern Marshall, a reflexologist from London. Fern. You were born in 1983. Liverpool were top of the first division – no premier league then – and beer was still served in pints. Tell us a bit about your earliest memories."

"Well," said Fern. Her mind went blank again.

"You were Joseph in the school nativity play, weren't you . . ."

"Mary." Fern giggled and the audience laughed. And then everything slotted into place as before, perfectly smoothly; she felt as though she was a cog in a very efficient machine, an important cog, and she was beginning to enjoy it. They got through Dermot and Frankie and Max.

He left out Karl and went straight into the trouble she'd had finding work, her failed marriage, her current situation.

"How long is it since you've had a holiday, Fern?" said Spliff.

Fern sparkled with anticipation. "Oh, years."

Patsy was holding Eveline's arm as she shepherded her to the side of the set for her entrance. She felt Eveline flinch the moment she saw Fern. She wondered whether Eveline was reacting to Fern's appalling haircut or Fern herself. "Isn't that a lovely surprise?" whispered Patsy, just in case Eveline had mistaken Fern for a sheepdog: "Your daughter."

Eveline's face had gone white. She took a step back.

"You'll be all right," whispered Patsy, "everyone feels like that." She pushed her forward again. She could feel Eveline resisting. Her head made a few quick movements, like a bird.

"You and your mother aren't speaking at the moment, are you?" Spliff was asking.

Fern wasn't going to be caught without anything to say a second time, she'd been thinking about this one for ages. "Mothers are a bit like the curse," she said. "You don't really want them; but once in a while you're awfully glad they've turned up."

Everyone laughed and Fern felt ecstatic.

"Let's have a big hand for Eveline, Fern's mother," said Spliff, smiling, "because we're all awfully glad *she's* turned up . . ."

Patsy gave Eveline a fairly hefty shove in the small of the back, and Eveline had to take a step forward. Spliff and Fern turned to look at her and she found herself walking down the steps. She sat down next to Fern. Fern smiled at her; there was more than a hint of malice in it.

"Hello, Eveline," said Spliff. "I want to talk about Fern's childhood for a bit."

Eveline swallowed.

"Things were hard for you," said Spliff. "You were on your own in a foreign country with a child, you had a living to earn . . ."

Get it over with, thought Eveline. "I am an alcoholic," she said. "I haven't had a drink for seven years, but I still attend regular meetings at AA. I was a different person when Fern was young."

"Nobody's criticising you for it," said Spliff, "we're just painting the picture so that the audience can understand how things were when it happened."

"When what happened?"

"Do you remember Karl?" said Spliff.

Fern stiffened slightly.

"Vaguely."

"He lived with you for a few months," said Spliff.

"He used to take Fern to play tennis," said Eveline. "That's right. He bought her a tennis dress."

"How did you split up?"

"Oh," said Eveline, "he just went. One day I came back from work and he'd just gone, taken all his stuff." It suddenly occurred to her that all her friends at work would probably be watching this programme.

"Didn't you wonder why?"

"I must have done, I suppose."

"Well," said Spliff, turning to Harry's camera, "just how far are we prepared to go on *Missing Link*? We're prepared to go *all the way*, folks. Because we've got Karl here in the studio and he's going to tell us why he ran out on Eveline all those years ago."

Bruce let go of Karl's arm, and Karl walked down the steps and went and sat next to Eveline. Fern had gone as white as a sheet. I hope she's not going to be sick, thought Eveline dispassionately. She puked up all the time when she was a baby, and she carried on puking up throughout her childhood. I was always getting calls from the school because she'd thrown up over someone.

"Karl," said Spliff, "it's very brave of you to agree to appear."

"I'm not the same person I was when I knew Eveline," said Karl. "I was ill in those days. I take medication now." He showed Spliff his tablets.

Spliff turned to Eveline with a wry smile, which he quickly suppressed for the camera. "Eveline," he said, "a little while ago you said you were a different person too. Do you think people should be forgiven for things they do in what, to them, is a previous incarnation?"

Eveline looked at Spliff. "I really can't answer that," she said.

"Well," said Spliff, "we all realise that Fern's childhood wasn't ideal. But you hope she's forgiven you for it, don't you?"

I'm not sure how much I really care, thought Eveline. But she couldn't say that. What she said instead was, "Yes, any mother would."

"I think Karl is hoping you'll see it that way when he tells you why he left, all that time ago."

"*I* want to tell it," said Fern.

Spliff looked at Karl. Karl opened his hands in acquiescence and the gold signet ring winked like a hazard light.

Eveline was staring at Fern. "What? Tell me what?"

"Karl raped me," said Fern. "Loads of times."

There was total silence.

"I had an abortion," said Fern, "when I was fifteen."

There was a slight muttering in the audience that suddenly turned to silence again.

"This is appalling," whispered Bronwyn Price to Nicholas Creed.

"Haven't you ever seen the programme before?" he whispered back.

"Only the one about the blind woman in the wheelchair who was given a bungalow by a lottery winner who knew her as a child."

Fern had actually got a grip of herself quite quickly. She described the first night, the dinner, the persuasion, the subsequent occasions, the threats. Karl sat there impassively, taking it all. Eveline was just sitting very still.

When Fern had finished she looked straight at Karl and said, "How do you feel about it all now, you shit?"

"Terrible," said Karl, with considerable sincerity. "I can't tell you how sorry I am."

Eveline was thinking, is this why you hated me so much Fern, why didn't you ever say anything? It's too late now you see, we've drifted apart. I always thought you were astoundingly empty-headed for a child of Edward's, but perhaps you were just screwed up. It's too late, though. We have nothing in common now. If we ever had.

"So," said Spliff, "a contrite rapist. Does it help, Fern?"

"Actually," said Fern, "yes. Particularly if I'm allowed to kill him afterwards."

Spliff laughed softly. "Perhaps outright murder is the only thing we'll stop at on *Missing Link*. Because just when you all think it can't get any worse, it does. Karl, I think some sort of reparation is in order, don't you?"

"What?"

"Well," said Spliff, "you can't undo the harm that's been done. But Fern doesn't earn a fortune, and you've just come into a small sum of money, haven't you?"

Oh you bastard, thought Karl, very neat. For a moment he wanted to argue, then he saw the expression in Spliff's eyes and he remembered what he'd said . . . *I can make sure there's a lynch-mob waiting for you when you leave.* Spliff might be just a slimy little git, but he was a powerful one. Karl nodded. "Yes, of course," he said, "she can have it all."

Fern looked astonished. Then she looked pleased.

You shallow little cow, thought Eveline. How could you.

"Money," said Spliff. He leant back in his chair and looked at the audience. "Money has become our emotional currency, hasn't it? Ring this credit card number to give to this charity, buy a lottery ticket, send a rape victim on a holiday. Much less hassle than actually speaking to your next door neighbour and finding out why they're looking miserable. Much easier just to watch it all, this emotional stuff, second-hand, isn't it folks? We'll be putting up some phone numbers just before the break so that you too can support rape victims."

Spliff turned to Karl. "Thank you Karl," he said, "for being brave enough to come on tonight."

Karl got up and hesitated for a moment, as though he was wondering whether he ought to shake hands with any of them. Then he seemed to think better of it and went.

"And now," said Spliff, glancing at the clock,

"we come to the part that Fern's been waiting for so patiently."

Eveline bit her lip.

"Fern," said Spliff, "did your mother ever tell you who your father was?"

"No," said Fern, with a black look in her mother's direction.

"Eveline," said Spliff pleasantly, "do you think you have the right to withhold that sort of information from your daughter?"

Eveline didn't say anything.

Spliff said, "I'd like to take you back to when you were working for DDI."

Oh well, thought Eveline. She might as well know. I don't really care, to be honest. I didn't say anything when I was drinking because I was still angry. Fern was mine. He wouldn't have wanted her. Now I'm sober it all seems very far away, like a dream, and I don't want Fern either. I probably only kept quiet about it for the last seven years to annoy her.

"My boss was a research chemist called Edward Pierce," said Eveline. "I was twenty-three and he was forty-five. He's dead now."

Fern looked as though someone had just put the lid back on the biscuit tin.

"I knew he had a history of failed relationships. But there was something about him; he was kind, and he was perceptive . . ." She paused.

"Go on," said Fern, "I want to know."

"I discovered that he was covering up some

malpractice. It didn't fit the man, you see; I felt I'd been a lousy judge of character. And when the whole thing got hushed up and DDI just went on producing the stuff, I got really angry. But before that I'd realised I was pregnant – with Fern."

Fern was looking at her intently. It wasn't quite as bad as she'd expected – her father could have been anything couldn't he, a criminal, a junkie. Eveline hadn't been awfully choosy when Fern was young. Instead he had been a research chemist, a clever man. A man with money? A man with no descendants?

"Edward had never wanted children," Eveline went on, "and he offered me the best medical solution money could buy. I took the money and I left the country, but I didn't have the abortion."

"So Edward never knew about her?"

"No."

"And you never wanted to tell him? No thoughts of revenge?"

"I wanted *him*, not compensation," said Eveline. "And he felt so strongly about not having children that telling him I hadn't gone through with it . . . no, I couldn't do it. So many conflicting emotions you see, love, hate, betrayal . . ."

"Yes," said Spliff, "I can see that." He told her what he'd said about Edward being innocent.

Eveline felt numb. She'd hated Edward for so long on that particular score that she didn't know what to feel in the hatred's place. She felt as though something had been taken away from her, something dear to her.

Spliff was watching the clock closely now. "It's going to come as quite a surprise to you then," he said, "to hear that Edward Pierce did eventually father a child of his own free will."

He glanced to one side, and Jessica's self-portrait appeared on the screen. Eveline looked thunderstruck.

"That's me, isn't it?" said Fern. "When I was a teenager." She hadn't quite caught on yet.

"No," said Spliff. "It's your half-sister, Jessica Pierce. It was a self-portrait she did when she was eighteen."

Fern's mouth dropped open.

Spliff continued, "But anyone who's ever tried to draw a portrait will know that the strangest things sometimes happen. You get one little bit wrong and suddenly you're looking at a picture of your great-aunt Gertrude, or your mother, or . . . your half-sister. We'll be back after the break, folks, when Fern can meet the half-sister she never knew she had, our first guest, Jessica Pierce. But before we go, here are those numbers I promised you earlier . . ."

The light on Harry's camera went out. Spliff glanced up at Clive. Someone was fanning a script in front of his face.

Twenty-four

"How much did Sandra tell you?" said Tree's wife in her nasty nasal voice. "I know you're screwing her and I don't give a shit; what I do care about is your career. You're here to be the right man at the right time tonight, when Spliff fouls up, and you know he's going to, don't you? You wanted to be here to see it happen nearly as much as you want your job back for the next series – with Stuart Miller as the new presenter, I imagine? So how's it panning out?"

"OK," said Tree, "Clive's too scared to pull the plug in front of Potty Noodle. That's what Spliff's banking on, anyway."

"So Clive gets the chop for not stopping him, you get Clive's job . . . and what about Spliff?"

Tree looked sharply at her. "You haven't, have you?"

"What?"

"Slept with him."

"No," said Tree's wife, annoyed, "I haven't." But her mind flashed back to a party some months previously, when she'd been talking to Spliff on the veranda. She'd got him in a corner behind the clematis and she'd thought she was doing quite nicely until Spliff suddenly said, "Just remembered – got to see a man about an aardvark." She'd disliked him intensely ever since.

"OK?" said Patsy to Eveline, as she came off.

"I'd like to go now," said Eveline.

"What, home? Aren't you even going to stay for the end of the show?"

"I just want to get out of here," snapped Eveline. "That man should be shot."

"Karl?"

"Spliff." The hatred was still there, working its barbs into her. The focus had changed, that was all.

"I've always wanted a sister," said Fern. Spliff was looking at something on the last page of his clipboard. She leant over – but although she could see that it was some sort of drawing, she couldn't see any detail. "What's that?" she asked.

"Do you like art?" asked Spliff.

"I know what I like." She laughed.

"Do you like music, reading, theatre?"

"Not especially," said Fern, "but I watch a lot

of television."

Fern thought he looked disappointed about something. She couldn't think what. Watching television was one of his hobbies as well, according to the magazines.

"Were you watching the monitor when I went to the loo?" asked Jessica.

Prudence glanced at Louise-Marie; Louise-Marie smirked. Spliff had to have something good, she knew him too well – just when you thought the build-up was over there was always one little bit more . . . The moment Prudence ushered Jessica away she switched the programme back on and settled down to watch.

Rudolph slipped back into the studio, and sat on one of the empty seats in the front row. Spliff turned to look. When he saw the state of Rudolph's face he froze. Rudolph waved at him, and then gave him a thumbs-up. Spliff looked at him for a long moment; then he relaxed and turned back to Fern. "Did he ever hit you?" he said suddenly.

"Who?" said Fern.

"Karl."

Her face clouded for a moment. "He didn't make a habit of it, like some of the others. But yes, he did slap me a couple of times." She glanced at him.

"I'm glad you got hold of him, Spliff. It's kind of . . . put something to rest."

Jessica could see Spliff talking to Fern, and yes, Fern was the woman with the atrocious haircut she'd seen on the first morning. Her half-sister. How incredible. The lights went down; then the bloody music started, and Spliff turned to Harry's camera.

"Welcome back," he said. "It's time to introduce Fern and Jessica to one another, half-sisters, remember, who didn't even know of one another's existence until *Missing Link* ferreted it out."

Jessica walked down the steps again. She saw Spliff say something to Fern, and Fern stood up. They gave each other the expected peck on the cheek. Fern sat down again, nearest Spliff, and Jessica sat next to her. She saw with a shock that Fern's hands were exactly the same shape as her own.

"Gosh," said Fern, "I don't know what to say."

Jessica's painting was on the screen again. "Oh yes," said Jessica, "I can see the likeness."

"You'll have to tell me all about him," said Fern cheerfully, "my father, I mean. No, *our* father. I can hardly believe it, all these years of not knowing and now . . . a sister as well."

Jessica found to her annoyance that after barely a minute's acquaintance Fern was beginning to irritate her. She didn't want her there, she wanted to be sitting alone with Spliff, talking about anything and everything. She wanted the programme to stop *now*.

"Tell us about the holiday you had in Costa Rica," Spliff asked her.

Jessica started to talk, conjuring up the images that had so captivated her in the cloud forest, on the beach, at the top of the volcano.

"What did you love the most?" said Spliff.

"I don't know . . ." said Jessica. "The humming-birds, maybe."

"Spliff loves Wittgenstein," said Fern. She seemed to be lagging behind in the conversation.

Jessica grinned. "Didn't Wittgenstein change his position?" she said slyly.

"That's right," said Spliff, clearly struggling to control his laughter. "He was a defender before he changed to goal."

"My father's hero was Socrates," said Jessica.

"Socrates?" said Fern.

"Played for Brazil in the 1980s," said Spliff. "Had an excellent dialogue with the ball. Questioned everyone. Very different to Hobbes."

"You see, I've missed out on all that sort of thing," said Fern, "without a father round the place."

Jessica glanced away. It was the only way she could stop herself having hysterics. At the same time she was marvelling at how the sheer rush of adrenalin could take her from numbness to euphoria within the space of a few seconds.

"Did Aaron Klein have any visitors whilst you

were in Costa Rica?" asked Spliff.

Jessica relayed the incident with Consuela and the American girl faithfully, wondering yet again why it was so important. She was beginning to feel all right, things weren't too bad.

Fern looked slightly bored. Suddenly she said, "How would you have felt if you suddenly found out that Jessica was *your* sister, Spliff?"

Spliff hesitated for a split-second. Then he said, "Delighted, obviously."

Oh yes? thought Rudolph.

"I know I'm a lot older than most sisters are," said Fern to Jessica, "but I don't think age matters much."

"No," said Jessica.

"I'm thirty-seven," said Fern.

"It's an interesting age to be," said Jessica.

Spliff smiled and looked down at his notes.

"No, it isn't," said Fern, "I'd love to be twenty-two again."

"Would you do things differently?" said Jessica.

"Oh yes," said Fern. "I'd study stage make-up, it must be really rewarding. I'm fed up with feet."

The audience laughed, and Fern looked pleased with herself.

"Maybe Jessica really *is* his sister," said Prudence, watching the monitor in the make-up room. "It would explain an awful lot."

"Such as?"

"Well," said Prudence, full of her own importance, "he didn't sleep with her."

"Didn't sleep with her when?" said Patsy.

"Didn't you know?" said Prudence. "They didn't go back for a drink with everyone else yesterday, they went badger-watching down in Surrey."

"Maybe you're right," said Louise-Marie. "Maybe they are related. You know what that means, don't you?"

Prudence looked at her. "No. What?"

"He's going to make this one personal. He's going to have himself as a sort of third subject. A second missing link."

Twenty-five

Bronwyn had enjoyed the philosopher exchange between Spliff and Jessica, although at the same time it worried her. When had Jessica drawn that picture of him, and why had Spliff wanted Bronwyn to see it? To tell her that there was more going on than met the eye? Oh God, I hope Jessica didn't get involved with him, thought Bronwyn, it would make everything just about as frightful as it could possibly be.

"I think I know what you're wondering," said Nicholas under his breath. "But Spliff never sleeps with his guests. If you ask him why, he just says he doesn't take work home with him. I know some people hate him, but personally, I like him. He knows an awful lot about Mahler."

Fern was getting bubbly now. They were well into the last third of the show and things hadn't been all that dreadful. She'd enjoyed it, really. Apart from seeing Karl, but even that hadn't worked out too badly in the end. Maybe she was owed some inheritance, too . . . "I bet you had everything you wanted when you were a kid," she said to Jessica, "clothes, holidays in America, a pony . . ."

"I had a lot of books," said Jessica, "and I went to some interesting places, but I didn't have a pony."

"What about you, Spliff?" said Fern.

Spliff looked at the audience. They'd all relaxed a lot since Eveline and Karl had left, and they'd had a few laughs. *Missing Link* was going more true to form.

"You don't want to know about my childhood," said Spliff, "do you?"

Choruses of "yes we do" came from the audience.

"No, you don't," said Spliff.

The inevitable response. Jessica watched him gauging exactly how far to push it.

"Oh, all right," said Spliff eventually.

Jessica suddenly realised that she had no defences left. Spliff had the audience on his side now, they *wanted* him to get personal.

He turned to Harry's camera. "This evening's programme has interested me very much," he said thoughtfully. "I told you earlier about both my parents dying. I know people get knocked down by buses, but you can excuse accidents. What I can't excuse are the parents who decide to have children knowing they

207

may not live to see their offspring reach adulthood. Money buys things that should never be bought under any circumstances. Education, health . . ."

"You did all right though," interrupted Fern. "And you came from a sink estate. The one where that bloke was putting rats into Cornish pasties."

"You don't think I'd have ended up doing this if I'd *really* come from there, do you?" said Spliff. "My parents had money. Not as much as Jessica's, but enough to send me to public school." He smiled. "I read Philosophy at university."

There was a stunned silence from the audience.

"Money doesn't buy love though," said Fern.

"No," said Spliff, "it doesn't." He paused, surveying the audience. "My parents bought *me*. I've resented it ever since."

"Blimey," said Louise-Marie, in the make-up room. "What the hell does he mean? He did a piece on the slave trade only two weeks ago, and he never repeats himself."

"Search me," said Prudence. She looked round. "Where did Patsy go?"

"She had another guest to bring up," said Louise-Marie.

"Another one?" said Prudence. "Who?"

"No idea. Some bloke."

"Clive doesn't know about that one either,

does he?"

"No," said Louise-Marie.

"What do you mean," said Jessica, "your parents *bought* you?"

"My parents were very close," said Spliff. "They were the sort of people who never should have had children at all, they only needed each other. They were married for eighteen years before they had me."

"Goodness," said Fern.

"They waited eighteen years because my mother bought every fertility treatment going. Eventually one of them worked. By that time she was fifty-one, and my father was ten years older. He died when I was six." Spliff glanced off-set. Jessica saw that Patsy was standing there, next to a small man with glasses and a roll-necked sweater.

"Consequently," said Spliff, "I have a bit of a thing about people who have children when there's a fighting chance the kid won't have any relatives left at all by the time it's grown up. We don't stop needing parents the moment we hit eighteen, do we? What I want to do now is to bring on our last guest of the evening, Dmitri Andropovitch."

The music started, a little late maybe, and Dmitri walked onto the set. Fern and Jessica moved up and he sat down next to Spliff.

"Hello Dmitri," said Spliff, "good of you to come. Tell us what you used to do for a living."

"I worked in clinic," said Dmitri.

"What sort of clinic?"

"We make babies," said Dmitri.

"A fertility clinic."

"Gynaecology clinic."

"You're retired now, aren't you? How long did you work there?"

"Thirty years. Was a good job. The ladies are so happy when they give birth after many years of trying."

"They don't all succeed though, do they?"

"Most of them get baby in the end. We can do such wonderful things now, Mr Spliff."

Spliff turned to the audience. "When I decided I was going to tackle this issue in an edition of *Missing Link* I contacted a number of clinics. I wanted a story that would illustrate just how I felt about it all. It took me a year to find one. I've lost count of the number of people I spoke to."

The camera moved in a bit.

"The medical professionals all closed ranks, of course," Spliff continued. "Patient confidentiality, or so they said. And a couple of promising stories turned into duds. Dmitri here was the guy who eventually came up with the goods, because Dmitri was a trained microbiologist, only no one would recognise his qualifications over here. So Dmitri just did the computer back-ups – which included the DNA profiles. And he kept them. You do that sort of thing when you have a background like Dmitri's. But Dmitri's history is another story altogether."

Dmitri smiled and nodded.

"It's just one of many such places," said Spliff. "All you need is the money to register. It didn't used to be like that. The one my parents used was in Italy, and they had endless paperwork to get through before they got what they thought they wanted. Tell me Dmitri, what's the procedure when a woman has trouble conceiving?"

"Well," said Dmitri, "you need to know whether there are the eggs; if there are the eggs, perhaps there is a reason they cannot reach the womb. The egg can be taken out, fertilised outside, and put back in the right place."

"And if there are no eggs?"

"She can have the egg from a donor."

"So the child has none of her characteristics, only those of the father – and another woman."

"But the wife grows the baby inside her. She loves him, it doesn't matter where the egg comes from."

"Doesn't it?" said Spliff.

"No."

"You said donor," said Spliff. "That kind of implies a gift. But it isn't, is it?"

"Is unpleasant process, extracting the eggs," said Dmitri, pulling at his collar. "The woman is paid. Why not?"

Spliff smiled. "Money again," he said. "Funny how it interferes with ethics, isn't it? Take television.

Once upon a time it was considered to be a public service."

Clive had left the box and come down to the studio floor. He was saying something to Harry. Harry pushed him away.

"So," said Spliff, "you pay the er . . . donor, the egg is fertilised by the husband, implanted in the wife and she carries it to term."

"Yes."

"Does the child ever know?"

Dmitri looked uncomfortable. "It is up to the parents to decide what they say."

"And just when, precisely, should they decide to do this?"

Dmitri shrugged. "Is different for everyone, Mr Spliff."

"I'll tell you when my mother decided to tell me," said Spliff. "The night my father died. I was six."

The audience was absolutely silent, riveted.

"I'll tell you about it, shall I?" said Spliff, with a quick glance at the clock. There were still a few minutes to go.

"When my mother told me my father had died she said she wished it was me and not him. She said I was going to be a constant reminder of what she'd lost, and there wasn't even any of her in me anyway. She told me she didn't know who my real mother was and she didn't care, it was only some cheap tart who needed the money. By the time I was seventeen my mother and I hated one another. I went out one evening when she'd told me not to, and when I came back she'd died of a heart attack."

Once again there was silence.

"After she died I tried to find out more, but the clinic had closed down and all the records had been destroyed. I have no idea who my biological mother was. No idea at all."

Twenty-six

Well well, thought Rudolph, all these years and you never bloody told me. You'll be headlines tomorrow, sunshine.

"We are what we are," Spliff was saying, "but we have to believe we have the power to change things. We're forgetting how to scream and shout when we see things that are . . . just plain *wrong*."

"Bloody hell," said Louise-Marie.

"Do you think he's been looking for his mother in all those different beds?" mused Patsy.

"Speak for yourself," said Louise-Marie. "He didn't behave like a dutiful son towards *me,* thank God."

"Tell me," said Spliff to Dmitri, "what sort of women

sell their eggs to infertile couples?"

"They don't sell to the couples," said Dmitri. "They sell to the clinic."

Spliff laughed. "A fine distinction, Dmitri," he said, "it allows for a profit margin doesn't it? And, after all, paying for them was the only way out. We all remember the sperm shortage – no one wanted to donate for free if their offspring became entitled to find them, and take them to court for maintenance. What a litigious society we've become. So how do they grade these eggs, Dmitri – IQ, common sense, artistic ability . . ."

"We don't accept anyone with hereditary diseases," said Dmitri.

"Is that all?"

"It depends how much you pay," said Dmitri.

"So I could have been an A minus egg or a D plus egg . . . depending on how much my parents were prepared to fork out."

"You put words into my mouth."

"It's my job," said Spliff.

The realisation had come over Jessica quite slowly. When Spliff turned to her she was not surprised, she just felt empty.

"Jessica," he said, "I'm sure you've been putting two and two together for the last few minutes."

She nodded, swallowed, nodded again. No allowances.

"We established that your mother was really

fifty-eight when you were born, not forty-five. Fifty-eight. And your father was sixty. Your father was definitely your father, but your mother had to be post-menopausal . . . you do realise that, don't you, the egg could not have been hers . . ."

"Yes," said Jessica, "I know. It all makes sense now. I'm the same as you." How very strange.

"Not quite," said Spliff.

"She's taken it well," whispered Bronwyn to Nicholas Creed. "I didn't expect her to take it quite so well."

"You knew then."

"I'd suspected. There was something about the mother – she wasn't *proud* of Jessica, and she should have been. I knew she was older than she said; she'd had a facelift, and she dyed her hair."

Nicholas noticed the streaks of white in Bronwyn's hair. "Silly thing to do," he said. "I think grey hair is very attractive." His own hair was nearly white.

"Yes," said Bronwyn, "I think so too."

"I asked you a bit earlier," said Spliff, turning to Dmitri again, "what sort of women sold their eggs to the clinic."

"No inherited diseases," said Dmitri.

"You said that."

"OK, OK," said Dmitri. "In the end it was

anyone, just about. Demand was greater than supply. We all know the fertility, she is declining all the time."

Fern seemed to have lost interest in the conversation, and was just sitting there staring at Jessica.

"So, what sort of women did you take?" persisted Spliff.

"Women who needed money."

"Women with children to support?"

"Yes."

"Women with drug habits to support?"

"No. No drugs."

Spliff leant forward. "Alcoholics? Did you ever take any alcoholics?"

Fern started to pay attention all of a sudden.

"Sometimes. It depend."

"Depended on what?"

"Whether they had . . ."

"Any inherited diseases," finished Spliff. "Yes, yes, what else?" He glanced at the clock again.

"Nothing else."

"Nothing else. Now tell us, Dmitri, what was the name of the man who ran your clinic?"

Dmitri looked around him. Then he looked back at Spliff. His boss had been a good man, yes, a good man, he had given Dmitri a job when no one else would.

"He is dead now," said Dmitri.

"His name."

No response.

Spliff said something softly in Russian.

Dmitri stiffened. "Aaron Klein."

Jessica felt quite numb now. Her father was still her father, but her mother wasn't her mother and so her aunt wasn't her aunt. She had a half-sister she didn't really want instead.

"You are one of my children," said Spliff. *"I am proud."*

Jessica looked at him. "Doctor Klein's last words to me," she said. "Yes. I see."

"He was an idealist, in his own way. He thought he was helping people."

Jessica took a deep breath. "You know who my biological mother is, don't you Spliff?"

"Yes."

He was going to do it. He was going to do something unspeakable to her in front of an audience of millions. Everything else had been a dream.

"Hey," said Fern unexpectedly, "so do I. I know who Jessica's mother is. Isn't that brilliant."

Spliff looked at her as though he could have killed her.

"It was what you said to Dmitri, wasn't it, about them using alcoholics. My mother was always short of cash. It's exactly the sort of thing she'd have done." She laughed out loud. "My mother is Jessica's mother as well, isn't she? So we're not half-sisters at all, we're full sisters."

Jessica felt sick.

Spliff turned to Harry's camera. "Well, folks," he said, "you've stayed with us so far, through a rather unorthodox edition of *Missing Link* – not quite the usual crap, anyway. And there's only another minute or so to go. So is this our missing link, the one we've all been waiting for – or can we turn the screw one more time?"

What? Maureen thought. What more can there possibly be?

Nothing more, surely, thought Bronwyn Price.

No, thought Rudolph.

Spliff turned back to Dmitri.

"You left out one very important fact when you told us about how the clinic obtained its eggs. Who else did you use, apart from miserable and desperate women?"

Dmitri mumbled, "Aborted foetuses. We performed abortions and used the eggs from the foetuses."

"Thank you," said Spliff. "It now becomes apparent that the tearful American girl must have been one of Aaron Klein's termination patients. He was still practising in Costa Rica." He turned to Fern. "What was the name of the clinic where you had your termination?"

"What?"

"When you were fifteen, twenty-two years ago. The name of the clinic."

"Oh. *The Warren.*"

Back to Dmitri. "And the name of Aaron Klein's clinic?"

"The Warren."

"And how old are you, Jessica? Twenty-two." Spliff turned to Harry's camera. "The last turn of the screw," he said, "and this week's *real* missing link. As we've already established, Fern is Jessica's half-sister, because Fern's biological parents were Eveline Marshall and Edward Pierce. Jessica's biological parents were Edward Pierce and the egg from an aborted foetus." He paused, but he didn't look away from Harry's camera.

Then he said, "That aborted foetus was Fern's."

He gave the audience a moment or two to digest this. Then he said, "So, you see, neither the woman Jessica knew as her mother nor her aunt are blood relations in any way whatsoever." He counted off the last four points on his fingers.

One. "Fern then becomes Jessica's *grandmother* as well as her half-sister."

Two. "Edward Pierce is both Jessica's father *and* her great-grandfather."

Three. "If Fern is Jessica's grandmother then *Eveline* is her great-grandmother and *Karl* is her grandfather."

Four. "Jessica's biological mother was *never born at all*. Isn't science wonderful?"

"My *God*," said Patsy, "that's so sick."

"Poor Jessica," said Prudence. "Fancy having a rapist for a grandfather."

"Hmm," said Louise-Marie, "poor old Jessica, more inbred than a pedigree pug." But she was thinking, Spliff did it, he strung her along – and then he skinned her alive. I wonder how she's feeling now . . .

Fern went a strange colour and put her hand to her mouth. Dmitri patted her absently on the arm.

Jessica just sat there, white.

Spliff leant forward, looking straight at Harry's camera, and spoke very fast. "Is this what you really want to see folks, people destroyed for your own amusement? Ever more sensational, ever more vicious, ever more voyeuristic? Are we really no more civilised than the audience in a Roman arena? Hasn't the time come to scream and shout a bit?"

Clive had completely taken leave of his senses and was struggling with Harry.

"Is this what you really want?" Spliff shouted at the camera. "Isn't it about time you started asking some questions? This wasn't what broadcasting was meant to be about. *Do something*, before it's too late, before we all become so inured to degradation and violence that we resurrect the Roman arena. We got rid of it once. Let's not bring it back. Let's remember that common sense and decency used to be part of our heritage. This will be the last time I present this show.

So goodnight, and let's hope *Missing Link* never runs again." The light on Harry's camera went out.

This was the moment when the audience was meant to start applauding. The assistant producer waved his arms at them, and mimed clapping. Nothing. The credits rolled; lights went out, other lights came on, and the audience started to talk agitatedly among themselves. Dmitri put his arm round Fern and led her away. She looked as though she was going to be sick again.

Jessica stood up.

"Fuck you," she said to Spliff, and walked off the set.

Twenty-seven

One year later, almost to the day, Nicholas Creed married Bronwyn Price. There were a lot of people at the wedding. The reception was somewhere down by the river, a huge house with extensive gardens going down to the waterfront. Sandra was there; she'd had a termination, told Tree to take a running jump, signed on for an MA and left television altogether. Prudence and Patsy were working on an out-takes programme. Patsy had a new hairstyle and some liposuction, and Prudence had a new veneer of sophistication – with the occasional lapse. Louise-Marie had got herself a job on a sit-com, and Clive had gone to America. There were no plans for another series of *Missing Link*.

It began to rain, nothing too heavy, just a little light drizzle, and people started to go indoors. Prudence saw Jessica walking away from her down towards the river. Prudence was higher up, and she could see that someone was sitting on the jetty, throwing stones into the water. Jessica wouldn't have been able to see him. Prudence was pretty sure that the someone was Spliff.

She started to run down the garden; she felt Jessica ought to know. As she turned the corner by the rhododendron an arm reached out and caught her by the wrist. Her shoulder jerked quite painfully as she skidded to a stop.

"Sorry," said Rudolph.

"I . . ." Prudence looked towards the river.

Rudolph shook his head.

"But she's going to . . ."

Rudolph shook his head again. "Leave them. It's taken me all afternoon to engineer this."

Prudence looked undecided.

"You can't cook *gigot à la provençale* by any chance, can you?" asked Rudolph.

Prudence laughed. "What a funny question. But the answer's yes, oddly enough. I worked on the last series of *Stuff It*."

Jessica just wanted to be on her own for a bit. She deliberately hadn't mixed, although she'd said hello to Rudolph. He told her he'd been to see the exhibition of graduate work, and he'd liked her stuff very much. He also told her there was a wonderful old willow down by the jetty she ought to take a look at. She wondered whether he'd just noticed that she needed to get away from everyone for a bit, and had given her a good excuse.

She came out from behind the bushes and realised with a shock that she wasn't alone. Someone was sitting on the jetty, with his back towards her and his legs hanging over the water. She heard her own sharp intake of breath. Sod you, Rudolph, she thought, and then realised that she'd said it out loud.

"I think you ought to know," said Spliff, without turning round, "that I can't swim."

She didn't say anything.

He was throwing stones at his reflection, one after the other; he had a little pile of them next to him. "I understand congratulations are in order," he said eventually, "on your degree. I found your work very . . . it had a lot of depth."

So he'd been to see it as well. He still had his back towards her. She still didn't know whether she wanted to push him in the river or not.

"It's quite deep here," he said.

The water was green and sluggish. The willow tree stood on the bank, trailing its branches between the flotsam. The trunk was split and twisted, thread upon thread of wood linked together in a beautiful linear complexity.

"Rudolph tells me," Spliff said slowly, "that I'm in love with you."

It was the last thing she'd expected. After a long pause she heard herself say, "And are you?"

"The trouble with Rudolph," said Spliff, "is

that the bugger's always right." He threw another stone into the water.

"Say it then."

He turned round, and the willow tree shivered in the rain. The two of them looked at one another for the first time in a year.

"Say it." Her face was as expressionless as his had been on the show.

He looked genuinely horrified. "What, without knowing how you're going to react?"

"Yes," she said, "without knowing how I'm going to react."

He stood up. Then he shrugged, spread out his hands and just said simply, "I love you."

"You only knew me for two days."

"No," he said, "*you* only knew *me* for two days. I knew you for six months." He took a step towards her.

"Oh no, you don't," said Jessica, stretching out her hands as if to ward him off, "I don't want any of that physical stuff clouding my judgement."

He stopped.

"So how did you feel after the show?" she said. "I want to know."

"Bloody."

"Is that all? Just bloody?"

"Very bloody. I felt unclean. No, I felt like a monster. You didn't think it through to the end, did you? I hadn't decided whether I ever wanted children. I can't now, can I? I've got ten fingers and ten toes, but who knows what's lurking in my genes?"

"Only what lurks in the children of first cousins," he said. "You'd need to find another cousin for things to go awry, and even then it's unlikely . . . Would you rather not have known?"

"Some days."

"And others?"

"You still don't realise, do you?" she shouted. "I now hate the people who brought me up! I used to love them. I'm selling the house because I hate that as well and I'm giving Fern half the money. My best friend Elspeth turns out to be a shallow little git. Maybe I knew that anyway. Maybe I only stayed friends with her because she was the nearest thing to a sister I had. *You* turned out to be someone who put principles before people – and in doing so you've taken away everything I had."

"No, I haven't," he said. "Your painting is more important than any of that."

"Yeah, did you notice the one of the embryo mother giving birth? Fern thought it was a sea-horse. Or the one of the psychopathic paedophile rapist? Lots of vermilion and black. My grandfather. That's the worst bit of all."

"Oh shit," he said, "I'm sorry."

"You're sorry. Terrific." She studied him. "But you'd do it again, wouldn't you? If you had the chance to go back in time you wouldn't do it any differently. It was one hell of a show, after all."

"I hoped that in the end . . . one day . . . you'd

understand."

"What exactly do you want from me?" asked Jessica.

"I don't want you to hate me." He glanced at her. "Purely selfish, as ever."

"I don't hate you *all* the time," she said, realising to her annoyance that she didn't, but cross with him for deliberately reiterating what he'd said just before he kissed her that one time.

"What do you feel then," he said, "when you're not hating me?"

I feel empty, thought Jessica. I need something from you, although I'm not quite sure what it is. But she just said, "Christ. You do push it, don't you? At one point I thought you were going to turn out to be my brother."

"I'm definitely not your brother. Different clinic." He scuffed a bit of gravel with his shoe. "I'm probably someone else's brother, somewhere. I'll never know."

"You can have Fern," said Jessica. "*I* don't want her. She keeps phoning me up and whingeing about her mother."

"Eveline's quite happy," said Spliff. "She's got a new hobby. Writing bitchy letters to newspapers about chat show presenters."

"Yes, I'd noticed. And Fern's got involved with some bloke who wrote to her after the show about his feet."

Spliff laughed. Then he said, "Actually, I don't

want a sister. I want you."

"Why?"

"For God's sake," said Spliff. "Are either of us ever likely to find anyone else who understands what this whole business feels like? I think what our parents did was wrong. Don't you think it was wrong? Forget all that I-wouldn't-be-here-otherwise crap, it's not the issue. The issue is whether this sort of genetic lucky-dip ought to be for sale. Don't you at least want to *talk* about it?"

She felt a bit guilty then. Spliff hadn't had it easy, either. Had his way of finding out about his ancestry been any better than hers? He ran his hand through his hair and looked at his fingers. She could see the water glistening on his palm. The rain was getting heavier.

She said, "So how did *you* feel about your past becoming public knowledge? I couldn't even go into a shop without people staring at me and whispering. It still happens. Somebody recognises me, and everything goes quiet."

"I'm used to being public property," he said, "I can cope with it. People think they know you, but they don't. They're only reacting to a reflection. Anyway, all that kind of got pushed under a whole load of other stuff."

"*Stuff?*" said Jessica. "A bit imprecise, for you."

"How many times do you want me to say it?" said Spliff. "I love you. And I'm not enjoying it very much. That runs true to form, at any rate."

"Maybe it's just that you can't get what you want for once."

He laughed. "I spent my whole childhood trying to get something I wanted, and I never succeeded."

"I suppose," said Jessica, "you think I ought to be grateful for what I had."

"You will be," said Spliff, "eventually. You can't do anything about what happened. It wasn't your fault. Don't let it spoil the rest of your life."

Jessica was shaking her head. "All those newspaper and magazine articles. Inaccurate, sensationalist – sadistic, even."

"Isn't that precisely what we were fighting?" said Spliff. "You can't trust the media any more, any of it. Photographs can be changed by computer, life histories deleted, overwritten, enhanced. If you don't educate people to look for the truth in the first place, you can't expect them to recognise the trash we put in its place."

"They called Aaron Klein Frankenstein. What does that make me?"

"You're looking at it the wrong way round. What does that make *them*?"

"Vampires, vultures, vipers . . ." said Jessica bitterly.

"Is that how you see me? As one of *them*?"

She bit her lip, annoyed. "No."

He hesitated, seeming to weigh her mood. Then he said, "There was a good one in *The Express*."

"What?"

"Spliff turns out to be a bad egg."

"Oh no." She couldn't help it; she laughed.

"You see," he said, "nobody else but you would be entitled to laugh at that one. One step forward?"

She didn't say anything.

He took a pace forward and stopped.

The stretch of wooden jetty between them was made of slats and she could see the water below. There were tufts of grass growing through some of them, doggedly persistent in the face of considerable odds. Survivors.

"In my defence," said Spliff, now very cool and measured, "I would like to call an owl as my first witness. This owl wishes to remind the prosecution that before he fell from grace he was once accepted as a friend."

"Underhand."

"But admissible?"

"All right."

He took another step forward across two of the wooden slats.

"I would like to cite drawing attention to the contents of the wineglass as being in the national interest."

"Fair enough."

One step.

He started to count on his fingers. "Badgers, Tit Willow, Escher . . . Damn. Should have used them separately, shouldn't I?"

She smiled. He stepped forward.

"There are some things," he said, "that art cannot serve."

"Such as?"

"Do you need me to spell it out?"

They were now about four paces apart. His eyes never left her face for a moment; she was reminded of a cat stalking a bird.

"Previous evidence of response in the prosecution whilst being kissed by the defence," said Spliff.

"Objection."

"Real or imagined?"

She didn't answer. She had suddenly realised that she actually wanted him, badly, and it was a shock. The feeling seemed to start somewhere in the small of her back and go right through to her fingertips. There was a slight change of expression in his eyes. He'd noticed.

"Overruled," he said quietly, taking another pace forward.

They were now within touching distance, but he made no attempt to close the gap between them.

"The defendant is contrite, and wishes to make amends the only way he knows how."

"How?"

"In bed."

"No beds here."

"Flowerbeds."

"Misrepresentation," she said.

He stayed where he was. "A lot in common. Striking similarities of background."

She nodded. He moved forward. They were now very close. The rain was running down her neck; she could see the water adhering like a fuzzy halo to his hair, she could have stroked it off with her finger.

"Finally," he said, after a long pause, "I would like to call on forensic science."

"Why?"

"It's a question of chemistry."

Jessica didn't have time to react on this occasion because he closed the gap. She felt the last thing she'd expected – an overwhelming sense of relief. She seemed to sink into him, as though she'd known his body for years. The feeling of relief was quite rapidly replaced by other feelings, however, and she forgot all about the rain, she forgot all about everything except what he was doing to her. It was he who eventually pulled away, and held her at arm's length. "Much more of that," he said, "and it *will* be the flowerbed. Shall we go?"

"Where?"

"Anywhere."

Why am I doing this, thought Jessica. I must be mad. Bronwyn will have a fit.

"I don't have a very good track record," said Spliff. "In fact, you're probably better off without me."

"I know that." But she didn't want to be with anyone else.

They walked back across the lawn, bodies linked together. Spliff suddenly stopped and said, "What do you reckon *The Mail* will make of this?"

Jessica looked at him. Then she took a deep breath and said, "An omelette, probably."

A Note from the Author

I started to write *Missing Link* a long time ago, before anyone had coined the term "Reality TV", or chat show sets had turned into Roman arenas. I got the idea after I'd agreed to appear on what was euphemistically termed "A Quiz Show", and I'd seen how the programme was put together to appeal to the lowest common denominator. When I tried to envisage how bad things could get, and follow this through to its logical conclusion, I needed another plotline. It was the perfect opportunity to write about a medical procedure that I believe is fundamentally *wrong*. I myself was the only child of elderly parents; it's something I care about rather deeply.

Book Club Questions for Discussion

1. Why is Rudolph so important to Spliff? Is it a typical male friendship? If not, why not?

2. Why do Fern and her mother have such a bad relationship? Is there anything that can be done about it, or is it beyond salvation?

3. During the run-through in the studio, Spliff asks what constitutes a nice man. Jessica replies: Someone who doesn't harm other people. Spliff then asks, What about someone who harms other people unintentionally?

Are people ever justified in doing the wrong thing for the right reasons?

4. Why does everyone seem to fancy Spliff, when he's not conventionally good-looking? Is power really an aphrodisiac? Or does he just have a way with women? What's his secret?

5. Why do people agree to appear on *Missing Link*, when they know their lives could be torn apart by it? Is it the lure of a possible windfall, or the craving for a brief taste of fame? Do people need to have their lives observed by others to feel worthwhile?

6. What is your opinion of reality TV shows? Is there any justification for laying bare people's lives in this way? Do you think the participants experience any long-term effects as a result of appearing on them? How does watching the genuine emotions of real people affect the viewer?

7. Spliff's official biography is very different from the reality. We know a great deal about some celebrities, and very little about others. Does this make a difference to how people feel about those in the public eye, and what they expect from them? What role do celebrities play in our lives?

8. Is Spliff right to be so antagonistic towards post-menopausal pregnancy? Are his reasons valid ones, and should there be exceptions?

9. How important do you think Jessica's ancestry should be to her? Do men and women have different opinions about this?

10. Should tissue from unborn foetuses ever be used, either for medical research or to enable an infertile woman to have a child? What are the long-term implications for a child conceived in this way? Should they ever be told about their origins?

A Death in the Family

Caroline Dunford

I briefly considered the option of swooning in a ladylike manner, but I was denied this by virtue of position: I was a maid; and by natural inclination: I have never known how to swoon. Instead I did what I believe most females of sensibility would have done finding themselves alone with a murdered corpse. I screamed exceedingly loudly, quite in the common manner, and pelted out of the room . . .

In December 1909 the Reverend Joshia Martins expires in a dish of mutton and onions leaving his family on the brink of destitution. Joshia's daughter, Euphemia, takes it upon herself to provide for her mother and little brother by entering service. She's young, fit, intelligent, a little naive and assumes the life of a maid won't be too demanding. However, on her first day at the unhappy home of Sir Stapleford she discovers a murdered body.

Euphemia's innate sense of justice has her prying where no servant should look and uncovering some of the darker secrets of the Stapleford family. All she has to defend herself with is her quick wits, sense of humour and the ultimate weapon of all virtuous young women, her scream.

Euphemia tells the tale in a light-hearted way, writing in a style akin to a cross between Jane Austen and Agatha Christie.

'A sparkling and witty crime debut with a female protagonist to challenge Miss Marple.'
Lin Anderson, Award winning Scottish crime author and screen writer

ISBN 978-1-905637-90-4 £6.99

PRINT
PUBLISHING

This Fragile Life

David Webb

Matt felt sick. He sank down onto a chair, the phone still clasped to his ear. He didn't speak for a few moments and Meg broke the silence.
'Are you still there, Matt? Are you all right? I thought you'd want to know.'
'Yes, thanks Meg. I'm coming in. I'm on my way.'
Matt put the phone down and sat still in the dark. Meg's words were echoing in his head and he was desperately trying to make sense of them . . .

Matthew Hudson is constantly reminded just how fragile life can be. Depressed by his routine existence in Manchester, Matt is haunted by the one failed relationship he has behind him – with Lydia, a dancer who left him to further her career in London. However, when he meets Laura, an attractive young primary school teacher, life seems to be looking up for Matt – until one phone call changes everything . . .

This Fragile Life is the first novel produced by prolific children's author David Webb.

ISBN 978-1-905637-87-4   £6.99

ePRINT
PUBLISHING

A Measure of the Soul

Stephanie Baudet

*The phone rang. Sighing, she went
back into the hall and picked it up,
lifting the earpiece to her ear.*

'Hello?'

*'I see they didn't find him,' said a voice.
'You obviously have him well hidden.'*

Harriet gasped. 'Who is this?' [. . .]

*'Did you really think you could hide
a deserter? How naïve you are,
Miss Baker.'*

For Harriet Baker, looking after her ailing father is a
distressing burden but after his death she is faced with
more problems and must cope alone.

It is 1918, the final year of the Great War, and when her
brother, Alex, goes missing while on compassionate leave,
she fears he will be shot for desertion.

Harriet hides him while the police search the house, never
sure just how he will react in his shell-shocked state,
and when he is seen by others, she is forced to yield to
blackmail and can confide in no-one, not even her best
friend, Gwen...

ISBN 978-1-905637-89-8   £6.99

PRINT
PUBLISHING

Spectacles

Pippa Goodhart

For days after that it was as if I'd died and gone to Heaven. The world was so full of beauty! . . . Seeing the world so clear felt like falling in love all over again . . .

When her domineering Mother dies, Iris is shocked by what she finds when clearing out her flat. It turns out that Iris is illegitimate. So she isn't the person she'd thought she was. Perhaps she can reinvent herself now?

When Iris acquires a pair of spectacles, she gains a renewed focus on life. She gives us her vision of the world around her, a clear, sometimes almost painfully comic view of people, places and the Meaning of Life! This complicated old woman shares some episodes from her life that move from gentle humour and pure farce to moments of tragedy and deep despair. Iris is always full of surprises, and she leaves the biggest surprise till the end of the novel, when she shocks the reader with the most poignant, eye-opening revelation of all.

'Throughout this potpourri of a novel, Goodhart writes with humour and pathos as we follow this wonderful old woman [...] on an emotional journey.'
Alan Wright, Author, nominated for the *Debut Dagger* Award

A moving story of life, death and all the questions in between.
Louise Heyden, Librarian

ISBN 978-1-905637-86-7   £6.99

ePRINT
PUBLISHING